Seashells and Seaweeds
by Roger Phillips

assisted by Nicky Foy
and Jacqui Hurst

Elm Tree Books London

INTRODUCTION

Aim

In the first section of this book we have aimed to photograph all the important and common shells that can be found on our coasts and, in the second section, we have photographed the important and distinctive seaweeds.

How to use this book

The shell section is divided into two main groups: the single shells (winkles, for example), followed by the bivalve shells (cockles, for example). In the seaweed section the plants are grouped by colour: first the green algae, then the red algae and finally the brown algae. Seaweeds are normally only found at a specific depth and generally we have dealt with those that are exposed by the retreating tide. These tidal levels are divided into three: the upper, middle and lower tidal levels. The upper tidal level is only covered completely by spring tides; the middle tidal level is covered and uncovered at every tide; and the lower tidal level is only uncovered completely by spring tides.

The photographs

The studio photographs were taken on a Bronica 120 format with a 75 mm lens. Scale: ○ is 1 cm. The field photographs were taken on a Nikon FM camera with a 50 mm lens, occasionally with close-up attachments. The film was Kodak Ektachrome 64 ASA in both cases, but when used outdoors it was pushed one stop in development. The underwater photographs were taken with an Olympus OM2 with 50 mm macro lens in Ikelite housing, using Kodachrome 64.

A collection of shells gathered from the beach

Glossary

alginate	jelly-like proteins extracted from seaweeds, used in processing food such as ice-cream
apical	at the top
byssus	threads by which some bivalves attach themselves to rocks
carapace	shell of a crab, an external skeleton
cardinal	main or most important
chiton	see page 4 (a type of shell)
dorsal plates	plates formed on back
filament	a thread
gill	organ by which underwater animals breathe, equivalent to lung in air-breathing animals
lunate	new moon-shaped
mantle	region of the body, in molluscs, which excretes the shell
operculum	opening or lid
periostracum	horny, thin, skin-like covering of fresh shell
sessile	without a stalk
siphonal canal	tube through which water is pumped into a shell
stipe	stalk
tubercle	small, warty growth
umbone	navel or oldest part of bivalve shell

Coat-of-Mail Chiton

Coat-of-Mail Chiton

Leptochiton asellus (synonym *Lepidopleurus asellus*) is found on rocks, stones, shells and coarse sand at the lower tidal level and below to about 150 metres deep. It is common in the English Channel, Atlantic and North Sea. Its maximum length is 2 cm. Note the mantle formed of eight, smoothish, fawny-grey or yellowish dorsal plates, encircled by a narrow fleshy girdle and 8 to 13 pairs of gills on the underside. Because of their articulating shell they can grip bumpy surfaces but if they become detached they roll up and come to no harm.

Callochiton septembvalvis is found under stones and on rocks at the lower tidal level and offshore. It is frequent in the North Sea, southwest Baltic, English Channel, Atlantic and Mediterranean. Its maximum length is 3 cm. Note the eight, smooth, shiny dorsal plates with the reddish brown 'eyes' (spots) on the first and last plates, encircled by a broad, fleshy, granular girdle. It has numerous gills on the underside.

4

Top three shells, *Lepidopleurus asellus*, bottom shells, *Callochiton septembvalvis*

Tonicella marmorea

Tonicella marmorea is found on rocks or stones at the lower tidal level and below. It is rare in the North Sea and North Atlantic. Its maximum length is 2.5 cm. Note the smooth, shiny valves, the pale girdle with very tiny, well spaced granules and the 19 or more pairs of gills. Its colour is reddish-brown with light patches. It is the largest British chiton. *Tonicella rubra* is similar but small and much more commonly found.

Lepidochitona cinereus is found under stones, on dead shells, and on rocky shores between the upper and lower tidal level. It is very common in the North Sea, southeast Baltic, English Channel, Atlantic and Mediterranean. Its maximum length is 2 cm. Note the finely granular, dull red, green or grey mantle of eight dorsal plates, encircled by a reddish brown or green fleshy ring. It has 16 to 19 pairs of gills on the underside. Like other chitons, it can roll up and survive undamaged if detached from its habitat.

Top lefthand-side, *Lepidochitona cinereus*, middle two shells *Tonicella marmorea*, bottom lefthand-side, *Tonicella rubra*

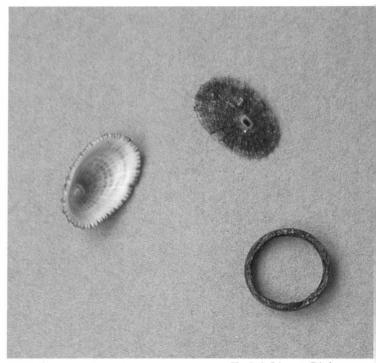

Keyhole Limpet, *Diodora graeca*

Green Ormer or Sea-ear

Haliotis tuberculata is found under stones and among rocks, in lagoons, at the lower tidal level and below to 13 metres. It is common in the Mediterranean and Atlantic as far north as the Channel Isles. Its maximum length is 10 cm. Note the flattened spiral and series of openings in mature shells and the thick inner lining of mother-of-pearl. Another species, **Common Ormer**, *Haliotis lamellosa*, is very similar though usually encrusted with algae. It's edible – eaten particularly in the Mediterranean.

Keyhole Limpet, *Diodora graeca* (synonym *Diodora apertura*), is found on rocks at the lower tidal level and below to about 20 metres. It is common in the southern North Sea, English Channel and Atlantic. Its maximum length is 4 cm. Note the yellow-white conical shell with a few, broad reddish or greenish-brown rays and 20 to 30 ribs radiating from the apical (keyhole) opening; from this a small tube protrudes when the animal is alive. Another species, Keyhole Limpet, *Diodora italica*, is grey-violet in colour and found in the Mediterranean.

Green Ormer or Sea-ear

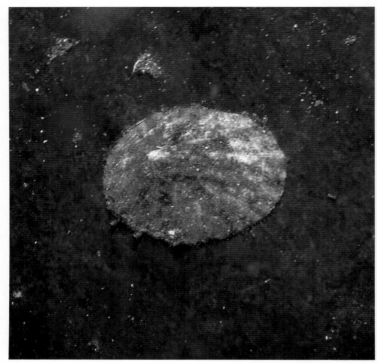

Tortoiseshell Limpet, *Collisella tessulata*

Tortoiseshell Limpet

Collisella tessulata (synonym *Acamaea tessulata, Acmaea testudinalis*) is found on small rocks and boulders at the lower tidal level and below to 50 metres. It is common in the North Sea, west Baltic and North Atlantic. Its maximum length is 3.8 cm. Note the flattened, white or greenish delicate shell and the reddish-brown markings which give rise to its name; also the characteristic chocolate-brown headscar inside the shell.

White Tortoiseshell Limpet, *Acmaea virginea*, is found at the lower tidal level and below to over 100 metres, particularly among the *Laminaria* group of seaweeds, and on dead shells and stones, and often on rocks encrusted with pink algae. It is common in the North Sea, west Baltic, English Channel, Atlantic and Mediterranean. Its maximum length is 1.25 cm. Note the smooth, delicate, cone-shaped, off-white shell with pinky-brown rays and the apex towards the front of the shell. It's difficult to spot because it is so small.

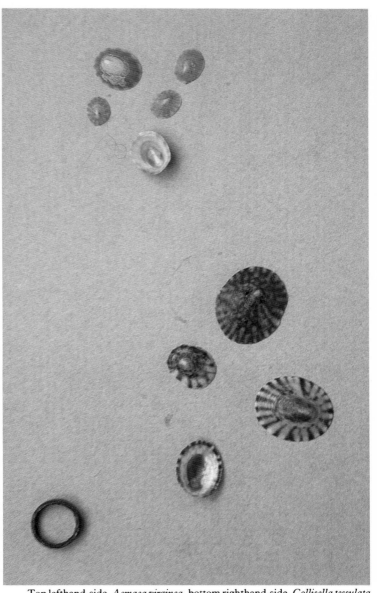

Top lefthand-side, *Acmaea virginea*, bottom righthand-side, *Collisella tessulata*

Common Limpet, *Patella vulgata*

Common Limpet

Patella vulgata is found on rocky or exposed areas on the middle and upper tidal levels. It is abundant in the North Sea, English Channel and Atlantic. Its maximum length is 7 cm. Note the tall, greeny-blue, grey or yellowish shell with irregular ribs, often barnacle-encrusted. Inside, the shell is white or yellowish with a silvery grey scar in the apex, and the mantle tentacles are transparent.

Patella depressa is intermediate between *Patella vulgata* and *Patella aspera*.

China Limpet, *Patella aspera*, is generally found in exposed areas on the middle tidal level to the bottom of the lower tidal level but also on the higher shore in weed-encrusted pools. It is common in the North Sea, and North Atlantic to southwest Britain. Its maximum length is 7 cm. Note the rather flattened, unmarked shell and white interior often with bluish iridescence, with cream or orange head scar, orange foot and cream mantle tentacles; it has finer and sharper ribs than *Patella vulgata*.

Top left corner, *Patella vulgata*, middle three shells, *Patella depressa*, bottom left corner, *Patella aspera*

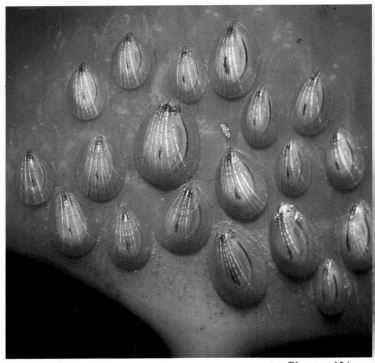

Blue-rayed Limpet

Blue-rayed Limpet

Helcion pellucidum (synonym *Patina pellucida*) is found on the lower tidal level and below to 27 metres, usually attached to the *Laminaria* group of seaweeds. It is very common in the North Sea, English Channel and Atlantic. Its maximum length is 2 cm. Note the smooth, golden-brown translucent shell with lines of vivid blue spots descending from the apex to the edge. These are usually much paler in older specimens.

Two subspecies are recognized: subspecies *pellucidum* (shown above) lives on the fronds of *Laminaria*, while the thicker and heavier subspecies *laevis* (shown bottom right) lives inside the holdfasts.

Blue-rayed Limpet, *Helcion pellucidum*

Toothed Winkle, *Monodonta lineata*

Toothed Winkle or Thick Topshell

Monodonta lineata is found on rocks and upper surfaces of stones at the middle tidal level. It is locally common in the west parts of the English Channel and Atlantic north to Anglesey. Its maximum width is 3.4 cm, height 3.0 cm. Note the thick, conical-shaped shell with six whorls, greyish green with zig-zag red-brown or green streaks. The mouth, lined with mother-of-pearl, has a single tooth. The top of older specimens is usually worn away, revealing a pearly yellow colour.

Gibbula magus is found buried in sand, in muddy gravel and under small rocks at the lower tidal level and below to 70 metres. It is common in the English Channel and Atlantic, south to the Mediterranean. Its maximum width is 3.5 cm, its height 3 cm. Note the solid, flattened shell with five or more irregular ridged whorls and knobs, a broad umbilicus, yellowy-white in colour variegated with red or purple streaks and stripes.

Upper shells, *Monodonta lineata*, bottom shells, *Gibbula magus*

Flat Topshell, *Gibbula umbilicalis*

Flat or Purple Topshell

Gibbula umbilicalis is found on rocks at the middle and upper tidal level and below to the top of the lower tidal level; it extends higher up the shore than *Gibbula cineraria*. It is locally very common in the English Channel and Atlantic. Its maximum width is 2.2 cm, height 1.6 cm. Note the flattened shell with about seven, barely ridged whorls, greenish-cream with broad red-purple stripes, and a larger more circular umbilicus than *Gibbula cineraria*. Another species, *Gibbula divaricata*, greenish with purple stripes, is found in the Mediterranean.

Grey Topshell or Silver Tommie, *Gibbula cineraria*, is found on seaweeds, stones and in pools on rocky shores at the middle tidal level and below to about 130 metres. It is very common in the North Sea, English Channel and Atlantic. Its maximum width is 1.5 cm, height 1.6 cm. Note the slightly less flattened shell with 5 to 6 whorls, greyish with thin red-grey bands, sometimes rather faded, running around the shell.

Top right corner, *Gibbula cineraria*, middle *Gibbula umbiliculis*, bottom right corner, *Gibbula divaricata*

Common Topshell, *Calliostoma zizyphinum*

Common Topshell or Painted Topshell

Calliostoma zizyphinum is found under stones and on rocks at the lower tidal level and below to 100 metres. It is common in the North Sea, English Channel, Mediterranean and Atlantic. Maximum height 3 cm, width 3 cm. Note the straight-sided, broadly conical shape with 10 to 12 shallow whorls with fine ridges, speckled yellowly pink with reddish-brown streaks. There are white, yellow and violet forms known.

Pheasant Shell, *Tricolia pullus*, is found in rock pools at the bottom of the lower tidal level down to about 38 metres, particularly among red seaweeds. It is common in the English Channel, south North Atlantic and Mediterranean. Its maximum width is 0.6 cm, height 0.9 cm. Note the glossy shell with five to six whorls, the bottom one over half the total height, with a yellowish white background and uneven, reddish brown markings. The operculum (lid) at the foot of the snail is white and shiny.

Large shells *Calliostoma zizyphinum*, small shells in bottom left corner, *Tricolia pullus*

Rough Periwinkle, *Littorina saxatilis*

Banded Chink Shell
Lacuna vincta is found on weeds at the lower tidal level and down to 40 metres. It is very common in the west Baltic, North Sea, English Channel and Atlantic. Its maximum width is 0.7 cm, height 1.25 cm. Note the pointed top and five to six smooth whorls, a shiny, semi-transparent, greenish-yellow in colour with distinctive red-brown bands.

Rough Periwinkle, *Littorina saxatilis*, is found in estuaries, mud flats, rocky cracks and crevices at the top of the middle tidal level and above. It is very common in the west Baltic, North Sea, English Channel, Atlantic and Mediterranean. Its maximum height is 1.8 cm. Note the six to nine, rough, rather deeply ridged whorls, ranging from red to black, and also the outer edge of the opening which meets the spire virtually at right angles.

Small Periwinkle, *Littorina neritoides*, is found in exposed rocky crevices above the upper tidal level in the splash zone. It is common in the North Sea, English Channel, Atlantic and Mediterranean. Its maximum height is 0.6 cm. Note the smooth, fragile, very pointed, blue-black shell. This is a lung-breathing winkle which feeds on lichens.

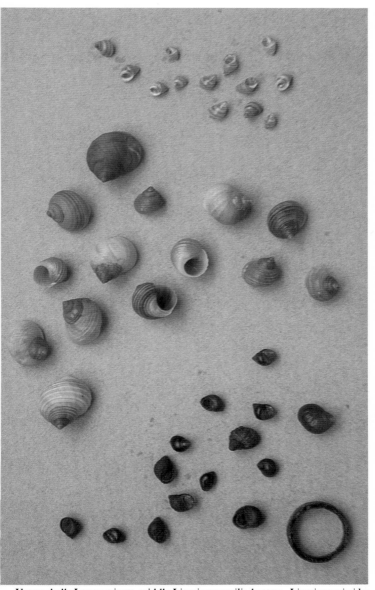

Upper shells *Lacuna vincta*, middle *Littorina saxatilis*, bottom, *Littorina neritoides*

Common Periwinkle, *Littorina littorea*

Common or Edible Periwinkle

Littorina littorea is found on stones, rocks, weeds, mud and sand at the middle tidal level and below to about 60 metres. It is abundant in the west Baltic, North Sea, English Channel, Atlantic and Mediterranean. Its maximum height is 3.4 cm. Note the solid, opaque, sharply-pointed shell with clear, dark-grey, brown or red sculpturing and concentric darker lines. This is a gill-breathing winkle which feeds on seaweeds. It is edible.

Flat Periwinkle, *Littorina obtusata* (synonym *Littorina littoralis*) is found on seaweeds (particularly *Fucus* and *Ascophyllum*) at the middle and upper sections of the lower tidal level down to 5 metres. It is very common in the west Baltic, North Sea, English Channel and Atlantic. Its maximum height is 1.5 cm. Note the rounded, virtually flat-topped shell, appearing smooth but in fact covered with very fine sculpturing. Its colour ranges from brown to red, green, yellow, orange. This is a gill-breathing winkle which feeds on seaweeds.

Top righthand corner, *Littorina littorea*, middle, *Littorina obtusata*, bottom lefthand corner, *Littorina mariae*

Laver Spire Shell

Hydrobia ulvae is found on mud in estuaries at the middle tidal level or in brackish water and salt marshes. It is common in the Baltic, North Sea, English Channel and Atlantic. Its maximum height is 0.6 cm. Note the elongated yellow-brown shell with about six whorls ending in a blunt top. It frequently eats sea lettuce and the left tentacle is thicker than the right. Another species, *Hydrobia ventrosa*, has fatter whorls, found in brackish creeks and lagoons. It is locally common.

Rissoa parva is found under stones and among seaweeds on rocky shores at the middle to lower tidal level and below to 15 metres. It is common in the west Baltic, North Sea, west English Channel, Atlantic and Mediterranean. Its maximum height is 0.7 cm. Note the pointed, ribbed shell, whitish-grey to fawn, with brown rays or bands, and the somewhat outward turning edge of the opening. It has a characteristic purple-brown comma shape by the apical part of the outer lip. Another related species, *Cingula cingillus*, has a banded shell and is found in crevices and in muddy gravel from the middle tidal level and below to 20 metres.

Top right corner, *Hydrobia ulvae*, middle, *Rissoa parva*, bottom right corner,
Cingula cingillus

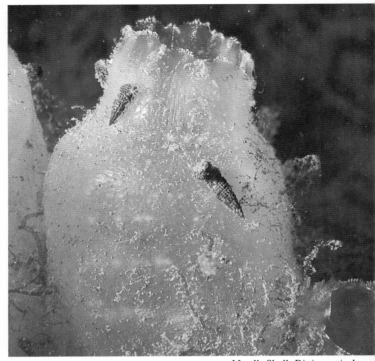

Needle Shell, *Bittium reticulatum*

Common Tower Shell or Screw Shell

Turritella communis is found buried in muddy gravel, soft bottoms or sand down from 10 to 200 metres, and empty shells are common on the shore. It is very common in the North Sea, English Channel, Atlantic and Mediterranean. Its maximum height is 6 cm. Note the narrow, conical, tapering shell with numerous, spirally-ridged whorls, ranging from red-brown to yellow or white, and its fairly small opening.

Needle Shell, *Bittium reticulatum* (synonym *Cerithium reticulatum*), is found on rocks, stones and debris and sometimes on sandy mud at the lower tidal level and below to 250 metres. It is common and locally very abundant in the west Baltic, North Sea, English Channel, Atlantic and Mediterranean. Its maximum height is 1.5 cm. Note the tall, narrow, reddish-brown shell usually with 10 to 12 whorls covered in rough nodules which are often worn smooth.

Common Tower Shell, *Turritella communis*

Pelican's Foot Shell, *Aporrhais pes-pelecani*

Pelican's Foot Shell

Aporrhais pes-pelecani is found burrowing in muddy gravel, sand or mud below low tide down to 180 metres, but empty shells are frequent on the beach. It is very common in the North Sea, English Channel, Atlantic and Mediterranean. Its maximum height is 5.4 cm. Note the yellowish grey, turret-like shell with many ornamental whorls. In mature specimens, the last whorl twists back at the opening and makes four jutting points, resembling a pelican's foot. The two groups of specimens are from different localities: the upper, more delicate, ones were trawled off Portugal; the lower, smoother two were dredged off Weymouth, Dorset.

Top five shells, *Aporrhais pes-pelecani*, were trawled off Portugal, the lower two were dredged off Weymouth, Dorset

American Slipper Limpet

Bonnet Limpet or Hungarian Cap Shell

Capulus ungaricus is found attached to rocks or other shells, usually bivalves such as Horse Mussels and Scallops, at the lowest tidal level and in deep water down to 850 metres. It is uncommon in the North Sea, English Channel, Atlantic and Mediterranean. Its maximum width is 5 cm. Note the wide, bonnet-shaped shell with its curved, pale top and darker, thick, brown periostracum, marked with concentric growth bands.

American Slipper Limpet, *Crepidula fornicata*, is found attached to oysters and other bivalves, and small stones in shallow water down to 10 metres. It is very common in the North Sea, English Channel and Atlantic. Its maximum length is 5 cm. Note the oval shell with its white interior and horizontal ledge. It is yellow, white or greeny-brown on the outside, sometimes with red marks and growth lines. This species lives in chains. There may be as many as a dozen in a chain: the top shells are young males, middle ones are changing sex, and the lower older members are female. It was introduced into British waters and is a prolific pest. It is edible.

Upper two shells, *Capulus ungaricus*, lower *Crepidula fornicata*

Velvet Shell

Velutina velutina is found at the lower tidal level in gravel and below, down to 1000 metres, feeding on Dead-men's fingers, *Alcyonium*. It is uncommon in the North Sea, English Channel, Atlantic and Mediterranean. Its maximum length is 2 cm. It was a whitish-pink shell comprising three whorls; the bottom one is very large, has a wide opening and is covered by a velvety, horny periostracum.

European Cowrie, *Trivia monacha* (synonym *Cypraea europaea*), is found under rocks and boulders feeding on compound sea-squirts at the lower tidal level and below. It is found in the North Sea, English Channel, Atlantic and Mediterranean. Its maximum length is 1.4 cm. Note the polished pink or purply-brown shell with about twenty pale-coloured ribs and three dark spots on the top, forming a slit-like opening underneath. When alive the shell is normally covered by the brightly coloured animal.

Trivia artica is found at the bottom of the lower tidal level and below to about 100 metres. It is uncommon in the North Sea, English Channel and Atlantic. Its maximum length is 1 cm. Note the slightly smaller shell, devoid of dark brown spots on the top, otherwise very similar to **European Cowrie**, *Trivia monacha*.

Pear Cowrie, *Cypraea pyrum* (synonym *Erronea pirum*), is found with seaweeds and under stones in deep water to 50 metres. It is frequent in the Atlantic south from Portugal and the Mediterranean, but is not present in British waters. Its maximum length is 5 cm. Note the glossy, red-brown shell dotted with darker marks which curves round to form a toothed, slit-like opening, paler red in colour.

Trivia monacha (top), *Trivia arctica* (middle), *Velutina velutina* (bottom)

Cypraea pyrum

Common Necklace Shell, *Euspira alderi*

Common Necklace Shell

Euspira alderi (synonym *Natica alderi*) is found burrowing in sand at the lower tidal level and below to 180 metres. It is common in the North Sea, English Channel, Atlantic and Mediterranean. Its maximum height is 2 cm. Note the shiny, smooth yellowish shell with 5 rows of red-brown spots or streaks on the body whorl. It has 6 to 7 whorls, the last expanding into a wide aperture.

Large Necklace Shell, *Euspira catena*, is found burrowing in sand at the lower tidal level and below. Its maximum height is 4 cm. Note the pale yellow, short-spired shell with reddish markings and seven whorls. It is similar to Common Necklace Shell, *Euspira alderi*, but it lacks the 5 whorls of spots.

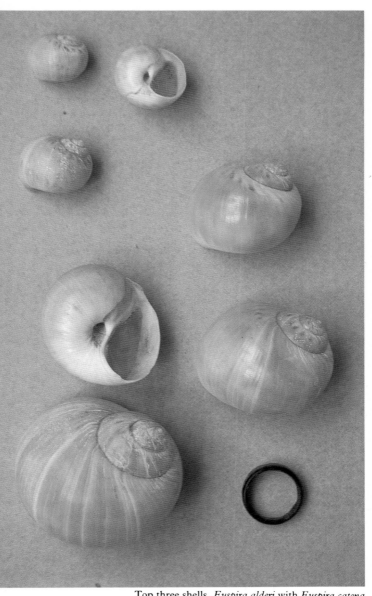

Top three shells, *Euspira alderi* with *Euspira catena*

Common Wentletrap, *Epitonium clathrus*

Violet Sea Snail
Ianthina exigua is found floating on the water's surface, using a 'buoy' of trapped air bubbles or occasionally on the shore after high winds. It is frequent in the Atlantic. Its maximum height is 1.7 cm. Note the beautiful, thin, violet shell, comprising about five whorls, lined with fine, V-shaped markings.

Common Wentletrap, *Epitonium clathrus* (synonym *Clathrus clathrus*), is found most commonly on muddy or sandy shores in water down to 80 metres, but also on rocks at the bottom of the lower tidal level during the spring spawning season. It is frequent in the west Baltic, North Sea, English Channel, Atlantic and Mediterranean. Its maximum height is 4.75 cm. Note the pale, spire-like shell, 2 to 3 bands of purple-brown streaks, with about fifteen deeply separated whorls and striking ridges, at right angles to the whorls.

Top two shells, *Ianthina exigua* with *Epitomium clathrus*

Sting Winkle containing hermit crabs

Common Dog Whelk

Common Dog Whelk

Nucella lapillus (synonym *Thais lapillus*) is found among rocks, in crevices or preying on barnacles and mussels at the middle tidal level, down to 40 metres. It is very common in the North Sea, English Channel and Atlantic. Its maximum height is 5 cm. Note the heavy, cone-like shell, varying from the usual off-white to yellow, or grey-banded with brown spirals. The outer edge of the opening is toothed in adult specimens. Grain-like egg capsules attached to one end are commonly found in crevices.

Sting Winkle or Oyster Drill, *Ocenebra erinacea* (synonym *Murex erinacea*), is found on sand, rocks, muddy gravel and under stones at the lower tidal level and below to 150 metres, spawning on shore between April and June. It is common in the North Sea, English Channel, Atlantic and Mediterranean. Its maximum height is 5 cm. Note the fairly pointed shell, yellowy cream with dark streaks, and 8 to 10 well-ridged, ribbed whorls. Its opening is toothed, with a siphonal canal in younger specimens. It feeds on bivalves by drilling through the shell.

Top three shells, *Ocenebra erinacea*, with *Nucella lapillus*

Spindle Shell, *Neptunia antiqua*

Common Whelk or Buckie

Buccinum undatum is found on sand or muddy gravel at the lower tidal level and below to about 1200 metres. It is common in the west Baltic, North Sea, English Channel and Atlantic. Its maximum height is 15 cm, though usually 8 to 10 cm. Note the large, brownish, pointed shell with well-ridged, ribbed whorls and a large, smooth opening with a short, siphonal canal. Empty shells, often inhabited by hermit crabs and spongy egg masses, are sometimes washed ashore. This Whelk is edible.

Spindle Shell, *Neptunia antiqua*, is generally found offshore although empty shells are sometimes on the shore, frequently inhabited by hermit crabs. It is common in the North Sea and North Atlantic. Its maximum length is 16 cm. Note the whitish, smooth-surfaced, spindle-shaped shell with very conspicuous ridged whorls and a long siphonal canal at the opening.

Common Whelk, *Buccinum undatum*

Dead Netted Dog Whelk with hermit crabs

Netted Dog Whelk

Hinia reticulata (synonym *Nassarius reticulatus*) is found in crevices, sand and mud or under stones at the lower tidal level and below to 15 metres. It is common in the west Baltic, North Sea, English Channel, Atlantic and Mediterranean. Its maximum height is 3.5 cm. Note the thick, brown, conical shell of about 10 whorls patterned with small, square ridges. This species is a scavenger on dead animals.

Thick-lipped Dog Whelk, *Hinia incrassata* (synonym *Nassatius incrassatus*), is found under rocks, stones or in crevices and muddy areas at the lower tidal level and down to 200 metres. It is common in the North Sea, English Channel, Atlantic and Mediterranean. Its maximum height is 2 cm. Note the small, brown, conical shell with darker bands, and a dark chocolate blotch on the base. It has about eight ribbed whorls which are well-ridged, and a thick-lipped opening; it has a short, siphonal canal. It is found in cleaner habitats than *Hinia reticulata*.

Top five shells, *Hinia incrassata*, with *Hinia reticulata*

Akera bullata

Actaeon Shell or Bear Barrel
Acteon tornatilis is found just buried in sand or mud at the lower tidal level and below to 250 metres. It is common in the North Sea, English Channel, Atlantic and Mediterranean. Its maximum length is 3.3 cm. Note the solid, glossy, rounded shell, of up to 8 whorls, pinky-brown with yellowish-white bands, and the elongated opening.

Akera bullata is found on mud flats or beds of eel grass. Note the thick, fleshy body wrapped around the shell and the long, projecting filament near the spire of the shell.

Canoe-bubble, *Scaphander lignarius*, is found in sandy or muddy substrates. It is common in the Atlantic, south from the English Channel and Mediterranean. The maximum length of the animal is 14 cm, shell 7 cm. Note the yellowy-white shell with the thin, reddish-brown periostracum and an opening that runs the length of it, tapering towards the tip. The white body of the animal is unable to withdraw into the shell.

Small shells, *Acteon tornatilis*, with *Scaphander lignarius*

Sea Hare, *Aplysia punctata*

Sea·Hare

Aplysia punctata is found among seaweeds, particularly *Laminaria*, in shallow water where it deposits long strings of orange or pink spawn. It is seasonally very common in the North Sea, English Channel and Atlantic. The maximum length of body is 20 cm. Note the thin, horny shell which is virtually covered by the red to browny-green body with four tentacles on the head. It squirts purple slime if disturbed. Two other, bigger, species, *Aplysia depilans* and *Aplysia fasciata*, are found in the Mediterranean.

Sea Lemon, *Archidoris pseudoargus*, is found in deep, rocky water or on the lower shore in the summer spawning season. It is very common in the North Sea, English Channel and Atlantic. Its maximum length is 7 cm. Note that this elliptical-shaped animal has no shell but two unbranched head tentacles at one end and an anus surrounded by a ring of nine, branching, retractile gills. Yellow, blotched with green, brown or pink, it has numerous small warts on its back and feeds on the breadcrumb sponge, *Halichondria*. It is the commonest of the British nudibranchs.

Sea Hare, *Aplysia punctata*

Sea Lemon, *Archidoris pseudoargus*

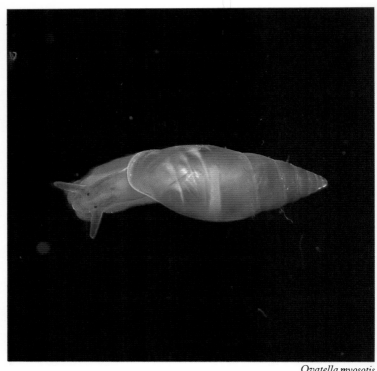

Ovatella myosotis

Leucophytia bidentata is found in estuaries and salt marshes, in crevices under small rocks and among old seaweed at the upper tidal level. It is common in the English Channel and Atlantic. Its maximum height is 0.8 cm. Note the solid, creamy-white, pointed shell with about six whorls and the two ridges on the inner wall of the opening.

Ovatella myosotis (synonym *Phytia myosotis*) is similar in size to *Leucophytia bidentata* but thinner and yellowish-brown in colour, and it sometimes has a third ridge on the inner wall of the opening.

Tusk Shell, *Antalus entalis* (synonym *Dentalium entalis*), is found in sand and mud from 6 metres down and occasionally washed ashore. It is common in the North Sea, English Channel and Atlantic. Its maximum length is 5 cm. Note the off-white, tusk-shaped shell which is slightly curved and tapering. A three-lobed foot, used for burrowing in sand, projects from the wider end of the shell.

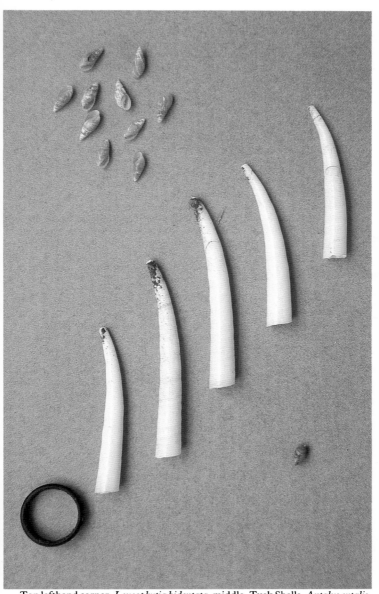

Top lefthand corner, *Leucophytia bidentata*, middle, Tusk Shells, *Antalus entalis*, bottom righthand corner, *Leucophytia bidentata*

Common Nut Shell

Nucula nucleus is found in muddy gravel, coarse sand or clay in shallow water and below to 147 metres. It is very common in the west Baltic, North Sea, English Channel, Atlantic and Mediterranean. Its maximum length is 1.3 cm. Note the similar valves with notched edges. The hinge line has more teeth in the front row than the back row. Its outer shell is greeny-brown or yellow or grey.

Cornered Ark Shell or Noah's Ark Shell, *Arca tetragona*, is found among stones and rock crevices, attached by a green byssus at extreme low water and below to about 180 metres. It is uncommon in the North Sea, English Channel, Atlantic and Mediterranean. Its maximum length is 6 cm. Note the similar, white-brown boat-shaped valves with finely sculptured grooves often obscured by calcareous growths. Its shell edge is notched at the back, smooth elsewhere.

Striaca lactea (synonym *Arca lactea*) is found occasionally between the tide-marks and more commonly offshore to 130 metres. It is common in the English Channel, Atlantic and Mediterranean. Its maximum length is 2 cm. Note the solid, dirty, yellowish-white shell with similar valves, sculpted with fine, radiating grooves and concentric ridges.

Dog Cockle or Comb Shell, *Glycymeris glycymeris*, is found burrowing in muddy or sandy gravel in shallow water and below to about 75 metres. It is common in the Baltic, North Sea, English Channel, Atlantic and Mediterranean. Its maximum length is 8 cm. Note the virtually circular, thick shell, with similar valves, yellowy-brown in colour with darker, zig-zag markings. Its edges are notched and it has two rows of 6 to 12 teeth on each hinge. It is edible. *Glycymeris pilosa*, violet in colour, is rarely found offshore in the Mediterranean.

Top left three, *Arca tetragona*, top right, *Nucula nucleus*, middle one, *Striaca lactea*, bottom, *Glycymeris glycymeris*

Common Mussels, *Mytilus edulis*

Common Mussels feeding

Common Mussel

Mytilus edulis is found on piers, stones and rocks in estuaries and exposed shores, often in dense beds, at the middle tidal level and below to 10 metres. It is abundant in the Baltic, North Sea, English Channel, Atlantic and Mediterranean. Its maximum length varies from 2 to 16 cm. Note the brown to purple or black shell with similar valves, smooth edges and pearly white interior tinged with mauve. It is edible, delicious.

Musculus discors is found under rocks and among seaweeds and small algae in pools at the middle tidal level and below. It is common in the North Sea, English Channel, Atlantic and Mediterranean. Its maximum length is 1.27 cm. Note the similar, thomboid-shaped valves and yellowy-brown shell. Its periostracum is greenish with generally smooth edges, which are however notched where the ribs meet. The front of the shell has about 12 ribs and the back area many more, although finer.

Common Mussels, *Mytilus edulis* with the small *Musculus discors*

Horse Mussel found on a beach near Stranraer, Scotland

Horse Mussel

Modiolus modiolus is found in rock pools and with the *Laminaria* group of seaweeds at the bottom of the lower tidal level and below to 150 metres. It is common in the North Sea, English Channel and Atlantic, south to the Bay of Biscay. Its maximum length is 23 cm but is usually about 8 to 14 cm. Note the thick, horny shell with similar valves; its periostracum which is purple or blue outside, white inside, with smooth edges and hinge line. It is edible, mainly eaten in Norway.

Bearded Horse Mussel, *Modiolus barbatus*, is found under rocks and shells and with the *Laminaria* group of seaweeds at the lower tidal level and below to 110 metres. It is common in the North Sea, English Channel, Atlantic and Mediterranean. Its maximum length is 7 cm. Note the thick, yellowy-brown periostracum which forms fringes of spiny whiskers, barbed on one side with bits of shell and sand sticking to it; it is otherwise similar to the Horse Mussel, *Modiolus modiolus*. It is edible.

Top lefthand corner, one *Modiolus barbatus*, with *Modiolus modiolus*

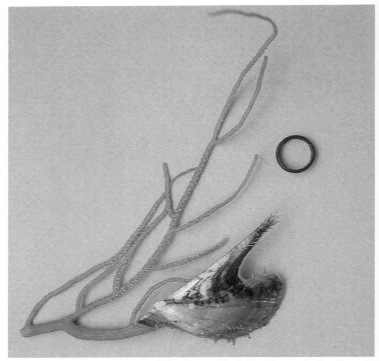

Wing Oyster, *Pteria hirundo*, attached to *Gorgorias*

Fan Mussel

Atrina fragilis (synonym *Pinna fragilis*) is found with its pointed end buried in mud, sandy mud or gravel, attached to small stones by its byssus threads, offshore to 160 metres. It is common in the English Channel and North Atlantic to Portugal. Its maximum length is 37 cm, maximum width 27 cm. Note the large, similar, fan-shaped valves with smooth edges, which are sometimes chipped. It is edible, delicious.

Wing Oyster, *Pteria hirundo*, is found attached to stones or *Gorgorias* on mud, clay or gravel offshore from 1 to 290 metres. It is common in the English Channel, and North Atlantic from Britain southwards, and in the Mediterranean. Its maximum length is 10 cm. Note the dissimilar valves with their strange, asymmetrical shape which form two protruding 'ears' at the hinge end, one very much larger than the other.

Fan Mussel, *Atrina fragilis*

Tiger Scallop, *Palliolum tigerinuma*

Tiger Scallop

Palliolum tigerinuma (synonym *Chlamys tigerina*) is found on sandy, gravelly or stony bottoms at the lowest tidal level and below to 95 metres. It is common in the North Sea, English Channel and Atlantic. Its maximum length is 2.5 cm. Note the solid, rounded shell with almost similar valves and protruding ears: the front one much bigger than the back one.

Variegated Scallop, *Chlamys varia*, is found either attached by a byssus thread to the substrate or swimming free, at the lowest tidal level and below to 1000 metres. It is common in the North Sea, English Channel, Atlantic and Mediterranean. Its maximum length is 8 cm. Note the solid, oval-shaped shell with slightly dissimilar, convex valves and protruding unequal ears: the front ones several times longer than the back ones. The shells are clearly ribbed, and are also notched with scale-like teeth. They are patchy in colour varying from white, pink or purply-red to yellow, green or brown.

The four smaller shells, *Palliolum tigerinuma*, with *Chlamys varia*

Great Scallop, *Pecten maximus*

Queen Scallop

Aequipecten opercularis (synonym *Chlamys operculans*), is found on firm sandy gravel or mud, attached by its byssus threads when young, but swimming free when adult at the lowest tidal level and below to 190 metres. It is very common in the North Sea, English Channel, Atlantic and Mediterranean. Its maximum length is 9 cm. Note the solid, rounded shell with almost similar valves and protruding equal ears, the front one only a little longer than the back one. It is very variable in colour, often with blotches, spots or stripes of many colours. It is edible.

Great Scallop or St James's Shell, *Pecten maximus*, is found in clean sand, fine or sandy gravel and occasionally muddy sand, offshore in shallow water and below to 1000 metres. It is very common in the North Sea, English Channel and Atlantic. Its maximum length is 16 cm. Note the solid, almost semi-circular shell with equal 'ears' and dissimilar valves: the upper are flat and reddish-brown, the lower are convex, cream or fawn with pinkish-brown markings. It is edible.

The four smaller shells, *Aequipecten opercularis*, with *Pecten maximus*

Common European Oyster, *Ostrea edulis*

Common European Oyster or Flat Oyster

Ostrea edulis is found on firm substrates of mud, rocks, muddy gravel, silt and commercial beds at the lower tidal level and in shallow water and below to about 82 metres. It is common in the North Sea, English Channel, Atlantic and Mediterranean. Its maximum length is 12 cm. Note the solid shell with dissimilar valves which can vary enormously in shape depending on the surface to which they are attached. The exterior, grey-green to yellow or brown shell is ridged and grooved with notched edges; the interior is pearly white. It is edible, excellent.

Portuguese Oyster, *Crassostrea angulata*, is found in commercial beds and on rocks and stones in muddy ground in shallow water. It is common, after its introduction from Europe, in commercial beds around Britain, and in the Atlantic, south to North Africa. Its maximum length is 18 cm, maximum width 7 cm. Note the solid, basically oblong-shaped shell, with dissimilar valves: the lower one is deeply cupped, the upper one flatter. The periostracum is brownish; the exterior dirty white, with deep folds

Upper shells, *Ostrea edulis*, with two *Crassostrea angulata*

Limaria hians

Common Saddle Oyster or Jingle Shell

Anomia ephippium is found attached to stones, rocks and other shells at the middle tidal level and below to 145 metres. It is common in the North Sea, English Channel, Atlantic and Mediterranean. Its maximum length is 10 cm. Note the dissimilar valves: the lower, thinner, flatter valve is pierced by a hole through which the byssus attaches the animal to the underlying surface; the upper, thicker, larger valve is more convex and circular. The valves often assume the shape of the object to which they are attached.

Gaping File-Shell, *Limaria hians* (synonym *Lima hians*), is found on bottoms of coarse sand or gravel, often among *Laminaria* seaweeds or in a 'nest' constructed by weaving its byssus threads among stones and sea weed, at the lowest tidal level and below to 100 metres. It is common in the English Channel, Atlantic and Mediterranean. Its maximum length is 3.5 cm. Note the thin-ribbed, white to dirty brown shell with similar valves which have a distinctive gap at the front.

The large shells, *Anomia ephippium*, with *Limaria hians*

Astarte sulcata

Astarte sulcata is found burrowing in muddy or sandy gravel and shingle offshore from 5 metres down to deep water. It is common in the North Sea, English Channel, Atlantic and Mediterranean. Its maximum length is 2.6 cm. Note the solid, white or salmon pink shell with similar valves, marked with numerous broad, concentric ridges. The brown periostracum has fine, concentric grooves undulating all over its surface and the inside edge is usually notched.

Goodallia triangularis (synonym *Astarte triangularis*), is found in sandy mud or gravel offshore to 95 metres. It is very common in the North Sea, English Channel, Atlantic and Mediterranean. Its maximum length is 0.3 cm. Note the solid, triangular-shaped shell with similar valves, white when worn, marked with very fine concentric lines. The light yellow to orange or brown periostracum has a few minute holes and the inside edge is notched.

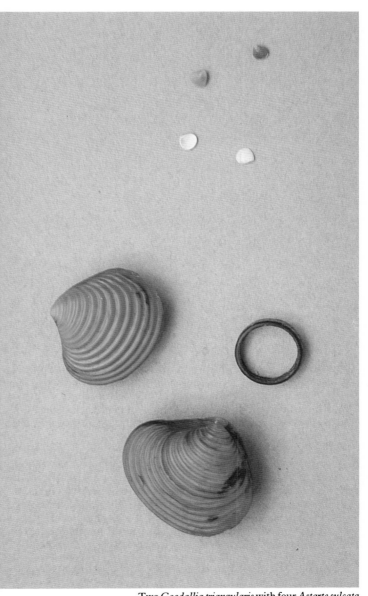

Two *Goodallia triangularis* with four *Astarte sulcata*

Prickly Cockle, *Acanthocardia echinata*

Prickly Cockle

Acanthocardia echinata is found in fine sand, mud or gravel, offshore from 4 metres downwards. It is frequent in the west Baltic, North Sea, English Channel, Atlantic and Mediterranean. Its maximum length is 8 cm. Note that the animal is yellow, white or pink, and that unlike Spiny Cockle, *Acanthocardia aculeata*, the left valve has cardinal teeth of similar size. In other respects these cockles are very alike. They are edible.

Spiny Cockle or Red Nose, *Acanthocardia aculeata*, is found more commonly in the Atlantic and Mediterranean. Its maximum length is 1 cm. Note the solid, plump shell with clearly defined ribs, each with rows of spines down the centre, and the characteristic red foot. It is edible.

Laevicardium crassum is found in muddy sand, broken shell and gravel in shallow water and below to 185 metres. It is common in the North Sea, English Channel, Atlantic and Mediterranean. Its maximum length is 7.5 cm. Note the solid, faintly oval-shaped, notched shell with similar valves sculpted in the middle with 40 or 50 very faint, smooth ribs. Its exterior colour is cream or pale yellow with red or brownish blotches and zigzags in young specimens; its periostracum is thin, greeny yellow or brown.

70

Upper shell, *Acanthocardia aculeata*, middle, *A. echinata*, lower *Laevicardium crassum*

Common Cockle, *Cerastoderma edule*

Common Cockle

Cerastoderma edule (synonym *Cardium edule*) is found burrowing in clean sand, mud or gravel at the middle tidal level and below into shallow water, also in estuaries and commercial beds. It is very common in the North Sea, English Channel, Atlantic and Mediterranean. Its maximum length is 6.2 cm. Note the solid, oval-shaped shell with similar valves and 22 to 28 radiating ribs bearing scale-like spines. It has notched edges with small grooves on the white shell interior. It is edible.

Lagoon Cockle, *Cerastoderma glaucum*, has a thinner shell which is somewhat triangular-shaped and smooth-edged at the back.

Little Cockle, *Parvicardium exiguum*, is found in gravel, sand or mud at the lowest tidal level and below to 55 metres, also in estuaries and brackish water. It is common in the North Sea, English Channel, Atlantic and Mediterranean. Its maximum length is 1.27 cm. Note the solid, plump oval shell with similar valves, each with about 21 radiating ribs, showing tubercles most predominantly in younger specimens.

Upper four shells, *Cerastoderma edula*, middle three, *C. glaucum*, lower *Parvicardium exiguum*

Rayed Trough Shell

Mactra stultorum (synonym *Mactra corallina*) is found burrowing in clean sand or gravel at the lowest tidal level and below to 100 metres. It is common in the North Sea, English Channel, Atlantic and Mediterranean. Its maximum length is 5 cm. Note the brittle, rather triangular, yellowish white smooth-edged shell with similar valves marked with fine, concentric lines and brown radiating rays. Two cardinal teeth in the left valve form a distinctive inverted V shape and the third tooth is separate, and often broken. Its anterior colour is white or purple. It is edible.

Elliptical Trough Shell, *Spisula elliptica*, is found burrowing in muddy sand or gravel and shell gravel at the lowest tidal level and below to 100 metres. It is common in the North Sea, English Channel and the Atlantic north from southern Britain. Its maximum length is 4 cm. Note the lighter, oval-shaped, smooth-surfaced shell with similar valves, marked with fine concentric lines. Its exterior is off-white; its periostracum is brown or greenish, its interior white.

Thick Trough Shell, *Spisula solida*, is found in sandy or gravelly bottoms at the lowest tidal level and below to 100 metres. It is common in the North Sea, English Channel and Atlantic. Its maximum length is 4.5 cm. Note the solid, dirty white, shell with similar valves, marked with concentric lines and grooves. It is similar to Rayed Trough Shell, *Mactra corallina*, except cardinal teeth are finely ridged instead of smooth. It periostracum is pale brown; its interior white.

Common Otter Shell, *Lutraria lutraria*, is found buried deeply in sand, mud or gravel at the lowest tidal level and below to about 160 metres. It is common in the Baltic, North Sea, English Channel, Atlantic and Mediterranean. Its maximum length is 14 cm. Note the thick, solid, oval-shaped, smooth-edged shell with similar valves, twice as long as their width. They are yellowy-white with a brownish green periostracum, and marked with concentric lines that do not meet at either end; the interior is white. It is edible.

Top three shells, *Mactra stultorum*, middle left, *Spisula elliptica*, middle right, *Spisula solida*, bottom left, *Lutraria lutraria*

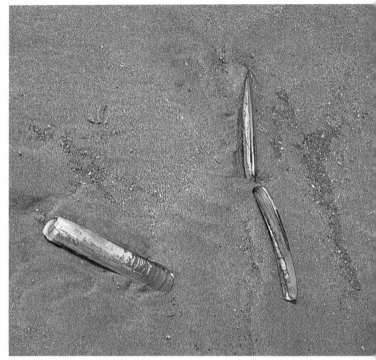

Pod Razor Shell, *Ensis siliqua*

Pod Razor Shell

Ensis siliqua, is found burrowing in clean, fine sand at the lower tidal level and below to 30 metres. It is common in the Baltic, North Sea, English Channel, Atlantic and Mediterranean. Its maximum length is 20 cm, width 3 cm. Note the long, narrow, brittle shell with almost straight, similar valves, gaping at both ends, marked with smooth, horizontal and vertical lines.

Ensis ensis is found burrowing in fine or silty sand at the lowest tidal level and below to 80 metres. It is common in the Baltic, North Sea, English Channel, Atlantic and Mediterranean. Its maximum length is 13 cm, width 1.9 cm. Note the narrow, curved, brittle shell with similar valves that gape at both ends and are marked with smooth horizontal and vertical lines. It is edible.

Ensis arcuatus is similar to both species but the shell is straight on the hinged side and curved on the other side, whereas the Pod Razor Shell is almost straight on both sides. *Ensis ensis* is curved on both sides.

Left to right: *Ensis siliqua, E. arcuatis, E. ensis*

Banded Wedge Shell, *Donax vittatus*

Grooved Razor Shell

Solen marginatus is found burrowing in sand or sandy mud to 18 inches at the lowest tidal level and below into shallow water. It is common in the Baltic, North Sea, English Channel, Atlantic and Mediterranean. Its maximum length is 12.7 cm, width 2 cm. It is similar to Pod Razor Shell, *Ensis siliqua*, but note the prominent vertical groove parallel to, and just behind the front edge. Its exterior colour is pale to dark yellow; its periostracum fawn; its interior white. It is edible.

Banded Wedge Shell, *Donax vittatus*, is found burrowing in clean, firm sand at the middle tidal level and below to about 20 metres. It is common in the Baltic, North Sea, English Channel, Atlantic and Mediterranean. Its maximum length is 4 cm. Note the solid, wedge-shaped, tooth-edged shell with similar valves. Its exterior colour ranges from white to yellow, purple or brown, sometimes with concentrated bands of colour and fine, pale radiating rays; its periostracum is green to yellow or brown. It is edible.

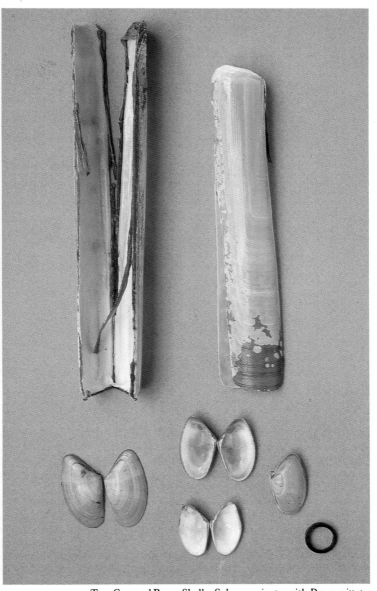

Two Grooved Razor Shells, *Solen marginatus* with *Donax vittatus*

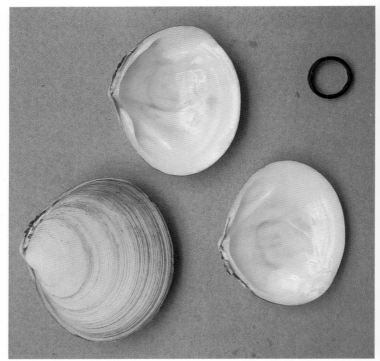

Blunt Tellin, *Arcopagia crassa*

Thin Tellin

Angulus tenuis (synonym *Tellina tenuis*) is found burrowing in fine sand, often in great numbers, at the middle tidal level and below to 10 metres. It is common in the Baltic, North Sea, English Channel, Atlantic and Mediterranean. Its maximum length is 2.5 cm. Note the brittle, flattened, smooth-edged shell with slightly dissimilar valves: its exterior colour is variable comprising concentric bands of yellow, orange, pink or white; its interior is similar; the periostracum is transparent and shiny. The strong external ligament often keeps the shell together after the animal has died.

Blunt Tellin, *Arcopagia crassa* (synonym *Tellina crassa*), is found burrowing in coarse or muddy sand and shell gravel in shallow water and below to 150 metres. It is uncommon in the North Sea, English Channel and Atlantic. Its maximum length is 6.5 cm. Note the solid, plump, oval to circular shaped, smooth-edged shell with similar valves. Its exterior colour is white to fawn; its periostracum is ochre, with concentric lines and radiating rays; its interior is red-orange with a white margin.

Upper shells, *Moerella donacina*, middle, *Angulus tenuis*, lower two, *Fabulina fabula*

Baltic Tellin, *Macoma balthica*

Baltic Tellin

Macoma balthica is found burrowing in thick mud, sand or gravel at the upper tidal level and below into shallow water and in estuaries. It is common in the Baltic, North Sea, English Channel and the Atlantic, south to Spain. Its maximum length is 3.5 cm. Note the solid, plump, smooth-edged shell with almost similar valves, marked with fine concentric lines of various colours ranging from white to yellow to pink or purple. Its periostracum is pale grey or colourless; its interior is white or mauve.

Gastrana fragilis is found burrowing in sand, clay or mud in shallow water and estuaries. It is rare and very local in the Baltic, south and west Britain, the Atlantic and Mediterranean. Its maximum length is 4.5 cm. Note the brittle, smooth-edged somewhat wedge-shaped shell with similar valves. The greenish-yellow shell surface is easily eroded and marked with irregular concentric ridges and fine radiating lines. Its periostracum is fawn; its interior white.

Upper shells, *Macoma balthica*, with three *Gastrana fragilis*

Peppery Furrow Shell, *Scrobicularia plana*

Large Sunset Shell

Gari depressa is found burrowing in coarse sand or mud at the lowest tidal level and below to 50 metres. It is common in the North Sea, English Channel, Atlantic and Mediterranean. Its maximum length is 7 cm. Note the solid, oval, smooth-edged shell with almost similar valves that noticeably gape at the back. Two similar species exist: *Gari fervensis* and *Gari tellinella* which is considerably smaller; their maximum length is 2.75 cm.

Peppery Furrow Shell, *Scrobicularia plana*, is found burrowing in soft clay, mud or sand from the upper tidal level and below to 2 metres, and in estuaries, tolerating low salinity. It is common in the Baltic, North Sea, English Channel, Atlantic and Mediterranean. Its maximum length is 6.5 cm. Note the oval, flattened, smooth-edged shell with similar valves marked with irregular concentric lines and ridges. Its exterior colour is pale yellow, brown or grey; its interior is white. It is edible.

Upper two shells, *Gari depressa*, middle four, *G. fervensis*, lower four, *G. tellinella*

Arctica islandica

Artica islandica (synonym *Cyprina islandica*) is found burrowing in muddy or sandy bottoms at the lowest tidal level and below to 200 metres. It is common in the west Baltic, North Sea, English Channel and Atlantic. Its maximum length is 13 cm. Note the solid, heavy, oval or circular-shaped shell with similar valves. The edge is smooth, the interior white, the periostracum thick, glossy and light brown to black with numerous, fine, concentric lines. It is edible.

Heart Shell or Heart Cockle, *Glossus humanus* (synonym *Isocardia cor*), is found on sandy or muddy bottoms offshore from 7 metres down to 80 metres. It is common in the Atlantic and Mediterranean. Its maximum length is 11 cm. Note the solid, plump, circular, smooth-edged shell with similar valves which look heart-shaped when viewed sideways. Its exterior colour is dirty white to fawn; and its periostracum is dark brown with fine, concentric lines; its interior is white. It is edible.

Upper shell, *Glossus humanus*, lower two shells, *Arctica islandica*

Warty Venus

Venus verrucosa is found burrowing in the top of sand or gravel at the lowest tidal level and below to 100 metres. It is common in the English Channel, Atlantic, and Mediterranean. Its maximum length is 6.5 cm. Note the solid, plump, rounded shell with similar valves clearly marked with concentric ridges which break up into wart-like spines towards the back. Its exterior colour is yellowy white to browny grey; its interior white. It has three cardinal teeth in each valve at the hinge. It is edible, eaten especially in France.

Irus irus (synonym *Notiris irus*) is found in holes and crevices of rock, particularly limestone, among the holdfasts of *Laminaria* and in very coarse detritus, at the lowest tidal level into shallow water. It is locally frequent in the west English Channel, and the Atlantic from south-west Ireland to North Africa and Mediterranean. Its maximum length is 2.5 cm. Note the brittle, white or fawn shell with similar valves, showing about 15 concentric ridges with frilly edges and thin radiating marks between them. The shell is often distorted to fit into a particular cavity.

Dosinia lupinus is found burrowing deep in sand, mud, silt or shell-gravel at the lowest tidal level and below to 130 metres. It is common in the North Sea, English Channel, Atlantic and Mediterranean. Its maximum length is 3.8 cm. Note the solid, round, smooth-edged shell with similar valves that form a 'lunale', a heart-shaped depression at the hinge, when closed. Its exterior colour is dirty white to yellow with fine concentric lines; its interior is white. *Dosinia exoleta* is a similar species with rays, zigzags or streaks of pink or brown on the outer shell.

Top left *Irus irus*, top right, *Venus verrucosa*, middle, *Dosinia lupinus*, bottom,
Dosinia exoleta

Banded Venus, *Clausinella fasciata*

Banded Venus

Clausinella fasciata (synonym *Venus fasciata*) is found burrowing at the lower tidal level and below 110 metres. It is common in the North Sea, English Channel and Atlantic. Its maximum length is 2.5 cm. Note the thick, solid, convex shell with similar valves that have broad, flat concentric ribs and numerous fine concentric lines. There are three cardinal teeth in each valve, at the hinge. **Striped Venus**, *Chamelea gallina* (synonym *Venus striatula*), has numerous, finer ribs near the ventral margin.

Banded Carpet Shell, *Paphia rhomboides* (synonym *Venerupis rhomboides*), is found burrowing in coarse sand or shell-gravel at the lowest tidal level and below to 180 metres. It is common in the North Sea, English Channel, Atlantic and Mediterranean. Its maximum length is 6.3 cm. Note the solid, smooth-edged, rather oval-shaped shell with similar valves, showing numerous smooth concentric rings and grooves. **Pullet Carpet Shell**, *Venerupis senegalensis* (synonym *Venerupis pullastra*), has concentric lines on the outer shell, crossed by fine, radiating lines.

Top left, *Chamelea gallina*, top right, *Paphia rhomboides*, lower two shells, *Venerupis senegalensis*

Blunt Gaper, *Mya truncata*

Blunt Gaper

Mya truncata is found burrowing in sand, mud or clay at the middle tidal level and below to 73 metres. It is very common in the North Sea, English Channel and the Atlantic. Its maximum length is 8 cm. Note the solid, cream or fawn shell with dissimilar valves; the left is less convex than the right and has a shallow, spoon-shaped projecting pit to which the internal ligament is attached. The valves gape prominently at the back, with a blunt posterior end. It is edible.

   Sand Gaper, *Mya arenaria*, is found burrowing in firm sand, mud or gravel at the lower tidal level and below to 73 metres, and in estuaries. It is very common in the Baltic, North Sea, English Channel and Atlantic. Its maximum length is 15 cm. It is similar to the Blunt Gaper, *Mya truncata*, but note the more oval shape and the fact that greater variation can occur in the texture, thickness and outline of this species. It is edible, good.

Sand Gaper, *Mya arenaria*

Common Piddock, *Pholas dactylus*, found at Sandwich Bay, Kent

Hiatella arctica is found boring into soft rock or nestling into existing crevices, attached by byssus threads at the lower tidal level and below into shallow water. Its maximum length is 3.5 cm. It is very common in the North Sea, English Channel, Atlantic and Mediterranean. Note the roughly oblong, irregularly-shaped, smooth-edged, yellowish-white shell with uneven concentric lines and valves which gape at the back.

Common Piddock, *Pholas dactylus*, is found boring into soft wood, rock, peat or firm sand at the lower tidal level and below into shallow water. It is frequent in the English Channel, and the Atlantic from south-west Ireland to north Africa and in the Mediterranean. Its maximum length is 15 cm. Note the brittle, white to grey, elliptical-shaped shell with similar valves, widely gaping at the front, with prominent criss-crossing ridges and ribs creating short, spiny projections. It also glows with a phosphorescent green-blue light in the dark. It is edible. **Oval Piddock**, *Zirfaea crispata*, is a similar species, but the shell is stubbier.

94

Top, *Hiatella arctica*, middle, *Pholas dactylus*, bottom, *Zirfaea crispata*

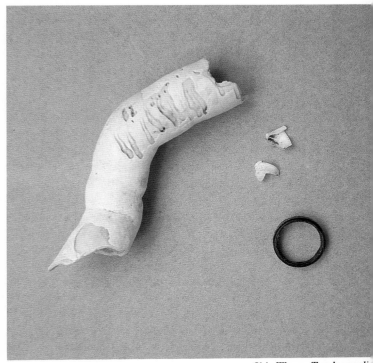

Ship Worm, *Teredo navalis*

Pandora Shell

Pandora inaequivalvis (synonym *Pandora albida*) is found in sand or mud in very shallow water and below to 5 metres. It is common in the North Sea, English Channel and the Atlantic. Its maximum length is 3.8 cm. Note the brittle, crescent-shaped shell with dissimilar valves: the left is convex, overlapping the right which is flat. Its exterior colour is white to pale yellow with faint concentric lines and undulations; its periostracum is fawn; its interior is pearly white with green tints.

Ship Worm, *Teredo navalis*, is found boring into submerged wood such as old boats or pilings. It is widely distributed in suitable habitats in the west Baltic, North Sea, English Channel, Atlantic and Mediterranean. Its maximum length is 1 cm. Note that the white shell acts as a drill, enclosing only part of the animal, and the mantle secretes a chalky tube, up to 20 cm long, which can be closed off by tiny, hard pallets, as the worm-like animal bores into the wood.

Pandora Shell, *Pandora inaequivalvis*

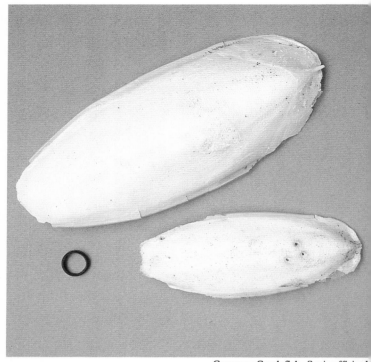

Common Cuttlefish, *Sepia officinalis*

Common Cuttlefish

Sepia officinalis is found in pools or among eel-grass in shallow water, and in bays or estuaries, spawning in midsummer. Sometimes the cuttlebone is found washed ashore. It is common in the North Sea, English Channel, Atlantic and Mediterranean. Its maximum length is 45 cm. Note the broad, rather flattened body with a conspicuous funnel under the head and 10 tentacles (2 very long) around the mouth. Colour very variable, depending on surroundings, often black and white striped or mottled. The internal shell, the cuttle bone, is enclosed in a shell. It is edible.

Little Cuttle, *Sepiola atlantica*, is found in summer either swimming over or burrowing in sand, just below the low-tide mark. It is common in the English Channel and the Atlantic. Its maximum length is 5 cm. Note the shortish, rounded body and the lobe-shaped fins which do not run its whole length. Its colour varies from black, brown or greyish above but usually pale below. It is edible.

98

Little Cuttle, *Sepiola atlantica*

Little Cuttle, *Sepiola atlantica*

Acorn Barnacles, *Chthamalus stellatu*

Goose Barnacle

Lepas anatifera is found attached to old boats and driftwood offshore on the sea's surface, although occasionally washed ashore. It is frequent in suitable habitats, in the North Sea, English Channel and Atlantic. Its maximum length is 5 cm. Note the shell comprising five, almost white plates with a dark blue translucent tinge and the long, partially retractable blue or brown-grey stalk.

Scalpellum scalpellum. Note the shell comprising 14 small, hairy greyish-white plates and the stalk covered in tiny scales.

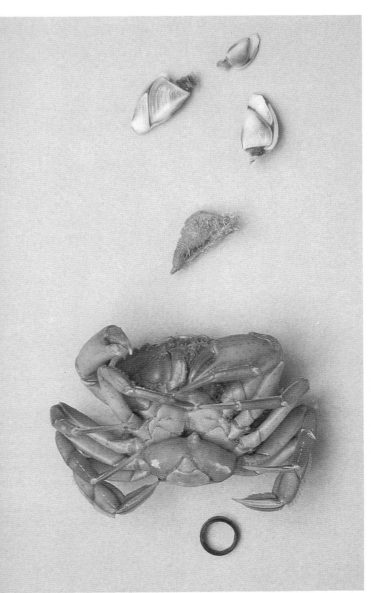

Upper shells, *Lepas anatifera*, middle, *Scalpellum scalpellum*, and *Sacculina carcini* on a shore crab, *Carcinus maenas*

Brittany Barnacles, *Balanus perforatus*

Parasitic Barnacle
Sacculina carcini is found attached to the common shore crab, *Carcinus maenas*, which lives in shallow water on sandy or rocky shores. It is common in the Baltic, North Sea, English Channel, Atlantic and Mediterranean. Its maximum length is 1.25 cm, width 2 cm. Note that this parasitic barnacle is unlike any other. It forms a smooth, yellowy, fawn-coloured lump under the abdomen and tail of its host, thus preventing the stomach from folding under the carapace.

Acorn Barnacles, *Semi balanus balanoides*, and *Chthamalus stellatus* are extremely difficult to tell apart but if both are present on the shore *Semibalanus* will be at the lower level.

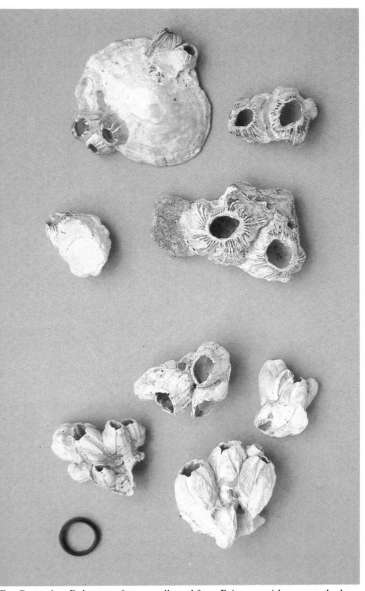

Top Barnacles, *Balanus perforatus*, collected from Brittany, with two attached to a limpet, with *Chthamalus stellatus*, gathered from Costa del Sol, Spain

Common Starfish, *Asterias rubens*

Feather Star

Antedon bifida is found on rocks or in crevices and under stones, in pools, at the lowest tidal level and below to 200 metres. It is frequent in the northern North Sea, English Channel and the Atlantic, north from Portugal. Its diameter is 15 cm. Note the five pairs of red-brown feathery arms which float sinuously in the water.

 Henricia Oculata (synonym *Henricia Sanguino lenta*) is found among pebbles and stones in soft substrates. It is frequent in the west Baltic, northern North Sea, English Channel and Atlantic, north from Portugal. Its maximum diameter is 25 cm but is commonly 8 to 15 cm.

 Common Starfish, *Asterias rubens*, is found on rocks and pebbly beaches, in oyster and mussel beds at the lowest tidal level and below to 200 metres. It is very common in the west baltic, North Sea, English Channel and the Atlantic. Its maximum diameter is 50 cm but is commonly 5 to 10 cm.

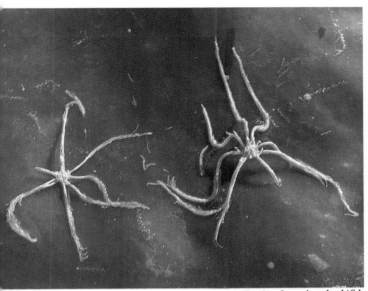

Feather Star, *Antedon bifida*

Henricia oculata

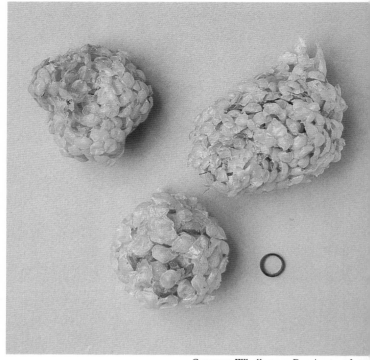

Common Whelk eggs, *Buccinum undatum*

Neptune Grass or Sea-Balls
Posidonia oceanica is found in the Mediterranean and Atlantic, south from Portugal. The broken leaves of this plant form soft, matted balls, and roll about in waves. Their diameter is 4 to 6 cm.

Sea Potato, *Echinocardium cordatum*, is a heart-shaped, spiny, sandy coloured urchin found burrowing in clean sand when alive, or its fragile whitish test (shell) may be found cast ashore.

Paracentrotus is a spiny, dark green or brown sea urchin, often covered with fragments of shell or seaweed, and sometimes found boring into rock at the lower tidal level and below to 30 metres.

Common Whelk Eggs, The eggs of *Buccinum undatum* form a large spongy-looking rounded mass of egg capsules, about the size of an apple, which often get washed ashore, but the individual egg cases will usually be empty when found.

Upper urchins, *Posidonia oceanica*, middle, *Echinocardium cordatum*, lower,
Paracentrotus

Marsh Samphire, *Salicornia europae*

Glasswort or Marsh Samphire

Salicornia europaea is found on open sandy mud in salt-marshes and estuaries, sometimes on sandy soils inland and occasionally on gravelly foreshores. It is common in the west Baltic, North Sea, English Channel and Atlantic. Its height is 15 to 30 cm. Note that this erect annual generally has several stems and opposite branches with shiny, succulent, jointed segments. The stem becomes rather woody by late summer and the plant turns from bright green to reddish. About nine similar but rare species of *Salicornia* can also be found. Lightly boiled in salted water, drained and served with butter and seasoning, marsh samphire is a delicious vegetable to serve with fish, eggs or meat.

Marsh Samphire growing on the mud flats of the Colne Estuary, Essex

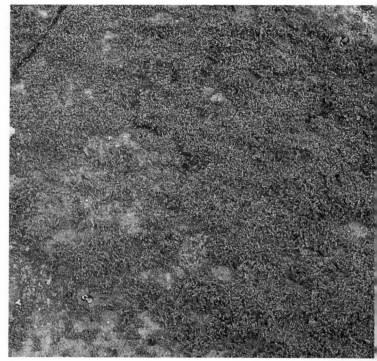

Prasiola stipitata

Sea Lettuce

Ulva lactuca is found at all times of year attached to rocks or stones at the upper tidal level and below to shallow water, or floating free in pools or washed up. It will tolerate a certain degree of fresh or polluted water. It is common in the Baltic, North Sea, English Channel, Atlantic and Mediterranean. Its length is from 15 to 50 cm. Note the wavy, translucent green, leaf-like fronds which vary in shape but often grow in bunches, giving rise to its common name. High in nutrients and trace elements, sea lettuce is sometimes eaten in Britain as a substitute for laver and highly valued as a culinary ingredient in many parts of the Caribbean, South America and Far East.

Prasiola stipitata is found on rocks at the top end of the middle tidal level. It is common in the North Sea, English Channel and Atlantic. Its length is 0.5 cm to 2.5 cm.

Sea Lettuce, *Ulva lactuca*

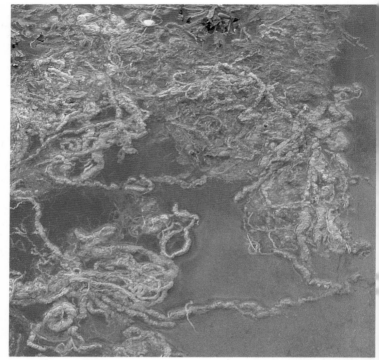

Enteromorpha intestinalis

Enteromorpha linza (synonym *Ulva linza*) is found attached to stones, rocks and other seaweeds in pools from the upper to lower tidal levels. It is frequent in the Baltic, North Sea, English Channel, Atlantic and Mediterranean. Its length is 10 to 50 cm. Note the thin, bright green, spirally twisted, unbranched fronds, with crinkled edges, which appear flattened but are, in fact, hollow.

Enteromorpha intestinalis is found throughout spring and early summer in rocky pools at the upper tidal level, in estuaries, salt marshes and brackish waters. The dead, bleached fronds are often found on the beach in late summer and autumn. It is very common in the Baltic, North Sea, English Channel, Atlantic and Mediterranean. Its length is 5 cm to 1 metre. Note the somewhat inflated, unbranched, translucent, pale green fronds which are contorted and constricted at irregular intervals.

Known in Japan as green nori and in China as tiger moss, it is valued as an excellent edible seaweed and used in numerous dishes.

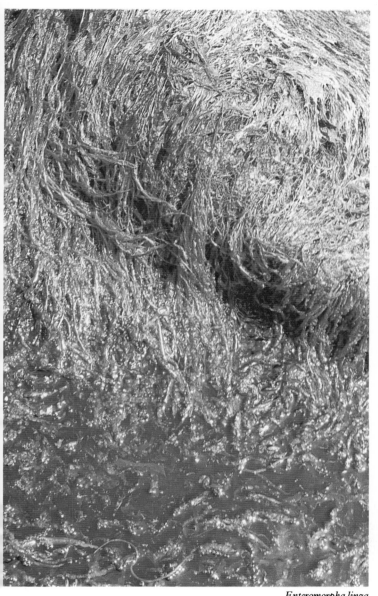

Enteromorpha linza

Blendingia minima   *Minostroma fuscum*

Cladophora rupestris is found at all times of year, growing on rocks and beneath large, brown seaweeds at the middle tidal level and below into deep water. It is common in the Baltic, North Sea, English Channel and Atlantic. Its length is 7 to 12 cm. Note the densely tufted, dark-green fronds with numerous, erect branches which look and feel rather harsh and wiry. Runners from the attachment base often start new growths and colonize large areas.

Blendingia minima (synonym *Enteromorpha minima*) is found on rocks, timber and other algae at the upper tidal level. It is frequent in the North Sea, English Channel and the Atlantic. Its length is 1 to 10 cm. Note the soft, delicate, green fronds which may be simple or slightly branched and sometimes inflated.

Monostroma fuscum is found in rock pools at the lower tidal level and below into shallow water. It is frequent in the North Sea and the Atlantic, north from the Irish Sea. Often mistaken for Sea Lettuce, *Ulva lactuca*.

Cladophora rupestris

Leathesia difformis

Leathesia difformis is found growing on rocks and other seaweeds, such as *Corallina*, at the middle tidal level and below from March to the end of September. It is very common in the North Sea, English Channel and the Atlantic. Its length is 2 to 4 cm; its width is 2 to 4 cm. Note the shiny, olive-brown, irregularly-shaped, rounded growths which are solid when young and hollow when old. They have thick walls and a rubbery texture.

Codium tomentosum is found on mud, sand, rocks or in deep pools at the middle tidal level and below to 20 metres. It is common in the North Sea, English Channel, Atlantic and Mediterranean. Its length is 22 to 37 cm in pools; up to 60 cm in deep water. Note the cylindrical, dark, yellowish-green, felty-textured fronds, with dichotomous branching, and the spongy holdfast comprising a mass of numerous closely-woven filaments.

A very similar species, *Codium fragile*, is known as chonggak or miru and is widely eaten either fresh or dried in Korea and Japan.

Codium tomentosum

Sugarwrack, *Laminaria saccharina*

Sea Belt, Sugar Kelp or Sugarwrack

Laminaria saccharina is found in rocky pools or attached to small stones, shells or rocks on muddy or sandy flats at the lower tidal level and below to 20 metres. It is very common in the North Sea, English Channel and Atlantic. Its length is 20 cm to 3 metres. Note the smooth, round, sandy-yellow stalk expanding into a single, long, flat, undivided frond with wavy edges and crinkled undulations all over it. The holdfast comprises several layers of branching fibres at the stalk's base.

Dried fronds have a whitish deposit on the surface which has a distinctly sugary taste and they are highly valued for their edibility, particularly in China and Japan. This seaweed is used by amateur weather forecasters has a guide to the humidity of the atmosphere.

Sugarwrack, *Laminaria saccharina*

Oarweed or Tangle, *Laminaria digitata*

Oarweed or Tangle

Laminaria digitata is found attached to rocks at the lowest tidal level and below to about 6 metres; it is often washed ashore. Sometimes large areas of it are exposed to the air for a short time, on slightly sloping beaches, during the low spring tides. It is very common in the Baltic, North Sea, English Channel and the Atlantic. Its length is 130 cm to 4 metres. Note the smooth, thick, cylindrical, flexible stalk which expands into a leathery, oar-shaped blade that divides into many ribbon-like fronds. The holdfast is comprised of numerous, intertwined, root-like fibres spreading over the rock's surface. Brown in colour it fades to green, then white, when exposed to the air for any length of time.

Fresh or dried Oarweed is high in nutrients and trace elements, and is often labelled Kombu when sold commercially. It makes an excellent addition to soups or stews.

Oarweed or Tangle, *Laminaria digitata*

Furbelows, *Saccorhiza polyschides*

Furbelows
Saccorhiza polyschides (synonym *Saccorhiza bulbosa*) is found attached to rocks at the lowest tidal level and below to 20 metres. It is common in the North Sea, English Channel and the Atlantic. Its length is 1.5 to 4.5 metres. Note the large, flat, wavy-edged stalk, twisted at the base but rather stiff towards the upper part, which grows out of a huge, knobbly, hollow holdfast that has small attachment roots. The stalk expands into a massive fan-shaped frond, divided into numerous ribbons. This is the largest seaweed found around Britain and is most common along the south and west coasts, although it only lives for one year.

Furbelows, *Saccorhiza polyschides*

Dabberlocks or Edible Kelp, *Alaria esculenta*

Dabberlocks or Edible Kelp

Alaria esculenta is found on exposed shores, attached to rocks at the lowest tidal level and below into shallow water. It is common in the North Sea and the northern Atlantic. Its length is 10 to 30 cm. Note the yellowish-olive stalk continues as the midrib of the long, thin, fragile, yellow-green frond, with wavy edges. This midrib is what distinguishes it from the *Laminaria* group which it resembles. The holdfast consists of spreading, root-like segments. The main stalk has many, short-stalked, swollen-ended outgrowths in which the spores are produced.

Known commercially as Wakame, fresh fronds and midribs are eaten in soups or salads or used as a thickener in many parts of the world.

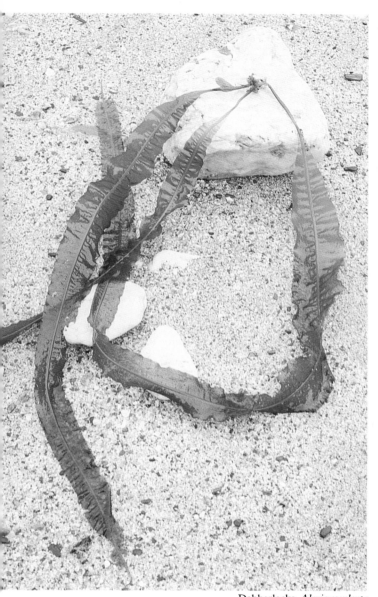

Dabberlocks, *Alaria esculenta*

Fucus ceranoides

Toothed Wrack
Fucus serratus is found attached to rocks at the lower end of the middle tidal level. It is very common in the Baltic, North Sea, English Channel and Atlantic. Its length is 60 to 180 cm. Note the tough, short-stalked olive green, branching fronds with thick midribs and serrated edges. In winter the tips have flattened, fruiting bodies growing from them. Small, white, spiral tubes of the worm *Spirobis* are often attached to older specimens.

    Fucus ceranoides is found attached to rocks and stones between the upper and lower tidal levels, in brackish water, and in estuaries and land-locked bays. It is common in the North Sea, English Channel and Atlantic. Its length is 30 to 60 cm. Note the thin, olive-green, dichotomously branching fronds with a distinctive midrib and clusters of forked, swollen tips which contain the reproductive bodies.

Toothed Wrack, *Fucus serratus*

Spiral Wrack, *Fucus spiralis*

Bladder Wrack

Fucus vesiculosus is found attached to rocks and stones at the middle tidal level, forming a distinct belt, and very small forms are sometimes found in salt marshes. It is very common in the Baltic, North Sea, English Channel and Atlantic. Its length is 15 to 90 cm. Note the numerously forked, tough, olive-green fronds with many edges and groups of two or three air bladders arranged either side of the distinctive midribs. Tips of the fronds have olive brown or yellow reproductive bodies.

Spiral Wrack or Twisted Wrack, *Fucus spiralis*, is found attached to rocks at the upper tidal level, often forming a distinct zone of about 1 metre. It is frequent in the North Sea, English Channel and Atlantic. Its length is 15 to 40 cm. Note the broad, tough, leathery, olive-green fronds which partially twist and have a distinctive midrib. The paler tips of the branches are swollen and contain the reproductive bodies but these do not extend to the rim, which is sterile.

128

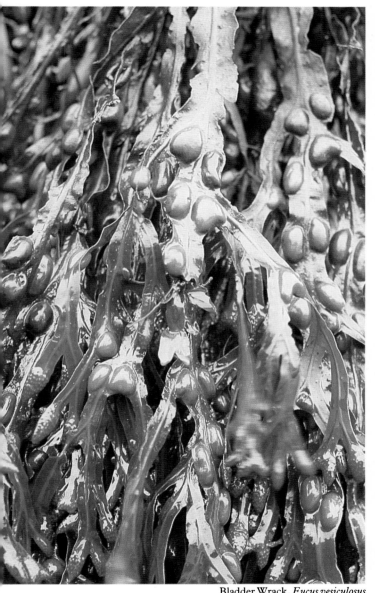

Bladder Wrack, *Fucus vesiculosus*

Knotted Wrack, *Ascophyllum nodosum*

Channelled Wrack

Pelvetia canaliculata is found attached to rocks at the upper tidal level, and above, where it forms a distinct belt, often only moistened by spray. It is common in the North Sea, English Channel and Atlantic. Its length is 5 to 15 cm. Note the tough, leathery, branching fronds, inrolled along the margins which enables moisture to be retained. The divided, swollen tips contain the reproductive bodies. It is olive to blackish green when dry.

Knotted Wrack, *Ascophyllum nodosum*, is found attached to rocks and boulders at the upper and middle tidal levels and can be very abundant on sheltered, rocky shores and estuaries. It is very common in the North Sea, English Channel and Atlantic. Its length is 30 to 150 cm. Note the disc-shaped holdfast from which the short, tough, dark-green stalks grow, developing into long, flat, leathery branches that fork repeatedly and produce egg-shaped air bladders. These are tough and not easily 'popped'.

Knotted Wrack contains algin and is used widely as an emulsifying or thickening agent in soups, puddings and jellies.

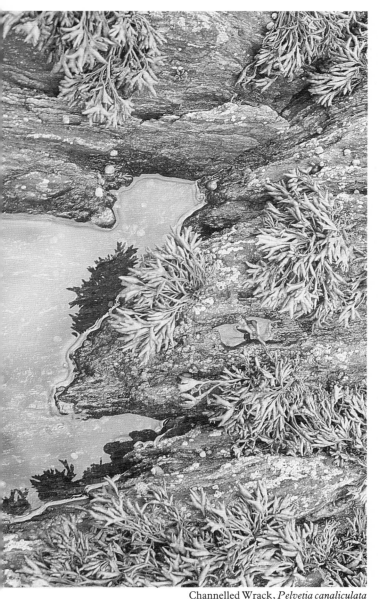

Channelled Wrack, *Pelvetia canaliculata*

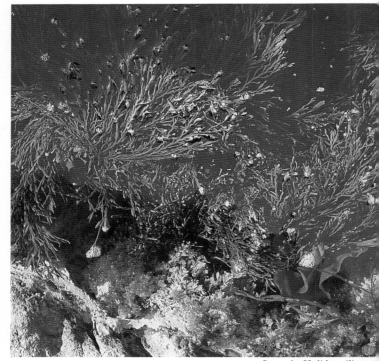

Sea-oak, *Halidrys siliquosa*

Desmarestia aculeata is found attached to rocks or stones in pools at the lower tidal level and below into shallow water; sometimes washed ashore. It is uncommon in the English Channel and northern Atlantic. Its length is 30 to 180 cm. Note the strong main stem bearing numerous alternately arranged side branches, covered with thorn-like branchlets which are bare in winter but covered with delicate little tufts in summer. It is bright green in colour, turning brown as the plant ages.

Sea-oak, *Halidrys siliquosa*, is found attached to rocks at the middle tidal level and below into shallow water. It is uncommon in the North Sea, English Channel and the Atlantic. Its length is 30 to 120 cm. Note the tough, leathery, rather flattened, olive-brown frond with regularly alternating side branches. The tips of the branches have long, pointed, oval-chambered air bladders rather like seed pods.

Desmarestia aculeata

Sea Lace, *Chorda filum*

Scytosiphon lomentarius is found attached to rocks, stones, shells and other seaweeds in rock pools at the middle tidal level and below into shallow water. It is frequent in the Baltic, North Sea, English Channel, Atlantic and Mediterranean. Its length is 15 to 30 cm. Note the shiny, greeny-yellow or brown, tubular, unbranched fronds, rather slimy to touch, with periodic constrictions that make them resemble a string of sausages. Short stalks join them to a disc-shaped holdfast. Several generations are produced each year growing lower and lower down the beach as the weather gets warmer.

Sea Lace, *Chorda filum*, is found attached to rocks and stones in shallow, gravel-bottomed water down to 20 metres. It is frequent in the Baltic, North Sea, English Channel and Atlantic. Its maximum length is 4.5 metres. Note the long, whip-like stems, unbranched and slimy, which grow from a small disc-shaped holdfast. Young plants are covered in fine hairs while the adult stems are hollow, tough and filled with air.

134

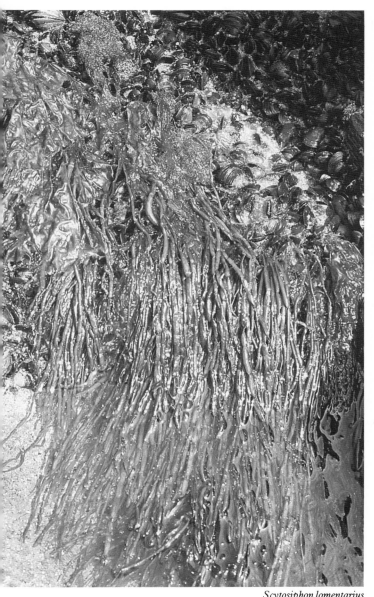

Scytosiphon lomentarius

Sea-thong or Thong-weed, *Himanthalia elongat*

Sea-thong or Thong-weed

Himanthalia elongata (synonym *Himanthalia lorea*) is found attached to rocks or growing in colonies in large pools at the lower tidal level and below into shallow water. It is common in the English Channel and the Atlantic Its length is 120 cm to 2 metres. Note the olive-green, mushroom-shaped buttons developed above the holdfast out of the centre of which grow long brown, leathery, strap-like branches which are forked and hang down wards. The spotty, reproductive parts of the plant develop on these in scattered pits. Sometimes the buttons will exist without the rest of the frond. As they become older they look like tops until they hollow out on the upper surface like a funnel.

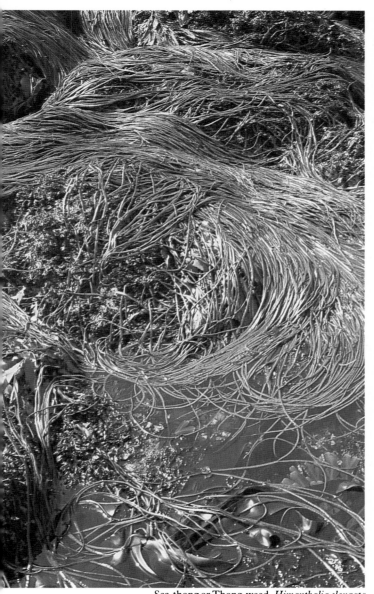

Sea-thong or Thong-weed, *Himanthalia elongata*

Laver, *Porphyra umbilicali*

Laver

Porphyra umbilicalis is found attached to rocks or stones in sandy places at all tidal levels. It is very common in the North Sea, English Channel, Atlantic and Mediterranean. Its length is 5 to 20 cm. Note the delicate membranous frond which grows in irregular, lobed leaf-like clusters attached at one point to a minute, disc-shaped holdfast. The rosy-mauve or purple colour turns olive green as it withers, then black and brittle when dry.

Cleaned, boiled until tender then cooked in oatmeal and fried in bacon fat, laverbread is a Welsh delicacy eaten all over the British Isles. It is cultivated for consumption in Japan by placing bundles of bamboo in shallow water offshore. Once the seaweed is established the laver-covered bamboo is transferred to brackish water in estuaries where it continues to grow, producing lusher, softer fronds.

Laver, *Porphyra umbilicalis*

Dulse, *Palmaria palmata*

Callophyllis lacinata is found attached to rocks, stones or *Laminaria* seaweeds in shallow water; it is also washed ashore. It is frequent in the North Sea, English Channel and Atlantic. Its length is 8 cm. Note the thickish, flat, forked, crimson frond broadening out from a very short stalk. In summer, reproductive bodies form in tiny growths at the frond's margin or over the whole surface.

Dulse, *Palmaria palmata* (synonym *Rhodymenia palmata*), is found on rocks and on the stalks of *Laminaria* and other seaweeds at the middle tidal level and below into shallow water. It is very common in the North Sea, English Channel and the Atlantic. Its length is 10 to 30 cm. Note the tough, blade-like, dark purplish-red, lobed and divided frond growing directly out of the wide, disc-shaped holdfast. Older specimens may have tiny 'leaflets' on the outer margins.

High in vitamins, and thought to have medicinal properties, dulse has a delicious, slightly salty, nut-like taste.

140

Callophyllis lacinata

Odonthalia dentata

Delesseria sanguinea is found attached to rocks or *Laminaria* seaweeds in deep, shady pools at the lower tidal level and below into shallow water. It is rare in the Baltic, common in the North Sea, English Channel and Atlantic. Its length is up to 40 cm. Note the crimson, wavy-edged, leaf-like fronds with clearly-defined midribs and conspicuous pairs of veins. The 'leaves' are attached to branched, rounded stalks growing from a small holdfast. In winter the fronds disintegrate and small spore outgrowths and leaflets develop along the midrib.

Odonthalia dentata is found attached to rocks, or sometimes other seaweeds, in pools at the lower tidal level and below into shallow water or cast up onto the beach. It is common in the North Sea and the Atlantic, north from Ireland and northern England. Its length is 7 to 30 cm. Note the main stem with rather solid, flattened, dark red, irregularly branched fronds tipped by shorter, toothed sub-branches and branchlets. The fronds have a distinct, peppery smell.

Delessaria sanguinea

Irish Moss or Carragheen, *Chondrus crispus*

Irish Moss or Carragheen

Chondrus crispus is found attached to rocks and stones at the middle tidal level and below into shallow water. It is rare in the Baltic, common in the North Sea, English Channel and Atlantic. Its length is 7 to 15 cm. Note that this seaweed can be very variable in form and colour but usually has either a distinct flat stalk or else a very short stalk with wide, flat, wedge-shaped fronds. These are generally purply-red, with lighter, iridescent tips, but turn green in sunlight. The margin of the frond is never inrolled, which distinguishes it from *Gigartina stellata*.

High in nutrients and trace elements, Carragheen is one of the most widely used edible seaweeds. Fresh or dried it is used as a vegetable in soups, stews, or as a thickener in mousses, jellies and desserts.

Irish Moss or Carragheen, *Chondrus crispus*

Gigartina stellata

Gigartina stellata is found attached to rocks and stones at the lower tidal level. It is common in the North Sea, English Channel and the Atlantic. It is 10 to 20 cm in length. Note the flat, tufted, dark red-brown fronds which fork six or seven times and are attached to a disc-shaped holdfast. These fronds have inrolled edges which form a channel. This and the small, fruiting 'pimples' which are dotted on older specimens, in summer and winter, distinguish it from **Carragheen**, *Chondrus crispus*. Old plants are often partially covered by a greyish-brown layer which consists of numerous colonies of a tiny marine animal, the **Sea-Mat**, *Flustrella hispida*. Edible, it can be used like Carragheen to thicken soups, stews and desserts.

Gigartina stellata

Calliblepharis ciliata

Cystoclonium purpureum is found attached to rocks and other seaweeds in pools at the lower tidal level and below into shallow water. It is common in the Baltic, North Sea, English Channel and the Atlantic. Its length is 15 to 60 cm. Note the root-like holdfast from which grows a thick, rounded stem about twice the diameter of the numerous branches which divide from it and then subdivide. All the branches narrow at their bases and taper to fine points at their tips. The whole plant is a dull, purplish-red which looks pinker in water.

    Calliblepharis ciliata is found attached to rocks in pools at the middle tidal level and below into shallow water, and washed ashore in spring. It is frequent in the English Channel and the Atlantic, south from Ireland. Its length is 15 to 30 cm. Note the holdfast comprising stout, branched 'rootlets' and the short stalk widening into a flat, blade-like, dark-red, pointed frond which sometimes divides in large specimens. Similarly shaped braches of varying sizes grow from the edges of the main frond.

148

Cystoclonium purpureum

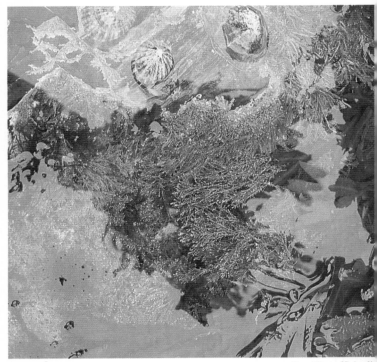

Corallina officinalis

Polysiphonia lanosa (synonym *Polysiphonia fastigata*) is found growing on *Ascophyllum* seaweed, occasionally on *Fucus* seaweed and very rarely on rock at the upper and middle tidal levels and in estuaries. It is very common in the North Sea, English Channel and the Atlantic. It is 8 cm in length. Note the tufts of dark red, thread-like branches which grow dichotomously at all angles from the strong main stem. Tiny red outgrowths on the plant are the algal parasite, *Choreocolax polysiphoniae*.

Corallina officinalis is found attached to roots just below the surface of rock pools or carpeting rocks in shady places at the middle tidal level. It is rare in the Baltic but common in the North Sea, English Channel, Atlantic and Mediterranean. Its length is 5 to 12 cm. Note the chalky, disc-shaped holdfast from which grow several dull purple, main stems with branches and further branchlets arranged exactly opposite each other. These comprise a minute series of calcified, bead-like segments which fade to yellow or white in sunlight.

Polysiphonia lanosa

Plocamium vulgare

Pepper Dulse

Laurencia pinnatifida is found attached to rocks and in crevices at the middle tidal level and below into shallow water. It is common in the North Sea, English Channel, Atlantic and Mediterranean. Its length is 2 to 30 cm. Note that the plant is rather variable in colour and size but mature specimens generally grow from a disc-shaped holdfast with rootlets, developing a strong, flattened main stem; while immature specimens grow in dense, crowded, yellowish-green tufts. The plant has a strong, distinctive smell and taste, as its common name implies.

Plocamium vulgare (synonyms *Plocamium coccineum* and *Plocamium cartilagincum*) is found attached to rocks or other algae in pools at the lower tidal level and below into shallow water; it is also washed ashore. It is common in the North Sea, English Channel, Atlantic and Mediterranean. Its length is 5 to 30 cm. Note the small, branching holdfast, supporting a strong, thick, rose-red stalk which branches regularly.

152

Pepper Dulse, *Laurencia pinnatifida*

Chylocladia verticillata

Lomentaria articulata is found attached to rocks and other seaweeds, in pools, at the upper tidal level and below. It is common in the North Sea, English Channel and the Atlantic. Its length is 5 to 25 cm. Note the tiny, disc-shaped holdfasts from each of which several hollow, branching stems grow. These are constricted at regular intervals giving a bead-like effect; at the constrictions one or several branches may divide. Spores form in pear-like structures on the upper branches. The shiny, transparent plant is dull-purple to crimson red in colour.

Chylocladia verticillata is found during late spring and summer attached to stones or rocks in pools at the middle tidal level and below. It is frequent in the North Sea, English Channel and the Atlantic. Its length is 15 to 30 cm. Note the hollow, articulated, main stem, growing from a small disc-shaped holdfast, which tapers towards its tip. Whorls of branches, similarly articulated and tapering, develop from each constriction in the main stem. Small, round, spore-producing growths develop all over the frond. Pinky mauve in colour, it turns yellow when exposed to the sun.

Lomentaria articulata

Lithophyllum incrustans

Phymatolithon calcareum is found either by itself or sometimes encrusting small stones at the bottom end of the lower tidal level and below into shallow water. It is frequent in the North Sea, English Channel, Atlantic and Mediterranean. Its width is 4 to 8 cm. Note the patch of thick, bumpy, chalky, violet-red growth which becomes erect with nodular branches as the specimen ages and resembles red coral.

Lithophyllum incrustans is found covering rocks on exposed shores at the middle tidal level and below. It is common in the North Sea, English Channel, Atlantic and Mediterranean. Its height is 4 cm. Note the thick, chalky, rough-textured, purple to pink or mauve crust which adheres closely to the surface on which it grows. Eight other similar but hard to differentiate species are found around Britain.

Phymatolithon calcareum

INDEX

Acanthocardia aculeata 70
    echinata 70
Acmaea virginea 10
Actaeon Shell 46
Acteon tornatilis 46
Aequipecten opercularis 62
Akera bullata 46
Alaria esculenta 124
Angulus tenuis 80
Anomia ephippum 66
Antalus entalis 50
Antedon bifida 104
Aplysia depilans 48
    fasciata 48
    punctata 48
Aporrhais pes-pelecani 30
Arca tetragona 52
Archidoris pseudoargus 48
Arcopagia crassa 80
Ark Shell, Cornered 52
    Noah's 52
Artica islandica 86
Ascophyllum nodosum 130
Astarte sulcata 68
Asterias rubens 104
Atrina fragilis 58
Banded Chink Shell 22
Banded Wedge Shell 78
Barnacle, Acorn 102
    Goose 100
    Parasitic 102
Bittium reticulatum 28
Blendingia minima 114
Buccinum undatum 42, 106
Calliblepharis ciliata 148
Calliostoma zizyphinum 20
Callochiton septemvalvis 4
Callophyllis lacinata 140
Canoe-bubble 46
Capulus ungaricus 32
Carpet Shell, Banded 90
    Pullet 90
Cerastoderma edula 72
    glaucum 72
Chamelea gallina 90
Chlamys varia 60
Chondrus crispus 144
Chorda filum 134
Chthamalus stellatus 102
Chylocladia verticillata 154
Cingula cingillus 26
Clausinella fasciata 90
Coat-of-Mail Chiton 4
Cockle, Common 72
    Dog 52
    Heart 86
    Lagoon 72
    Little 72
    Prickly 70
    Spiny 70

Codium fragile 116
    tomentosum 116
Collisella tessulata 10
Common Cuttlefish 98
    Necklace Shell 36
    Nut Shell 52
    Ormer 8
    Otter Shell 74
    Periwinkle 24
    Piddock 94
    Saddle Oyster 66
    Starfish 104
    Tower Shell 28
    Wentletrap 38
    Whelk eggs 106
Corallina officinalis 150
Cowrie, European 34
    Pear 34
Cuttle, Little 98
Crepidula fornicata 32
Cypraea pyrum 34
Cystoclonium purpureum 148
Dabberlocks 124
Delesseria sanguinea 142
Desmarestia aculeata 132
Diodora graeca 8
    italica 8
Donax vittatus 78
Dulse 140
Echinocardium cordatum 106
    Periwinkle 24
Elliptical Trough Shell 74
Ensis arcuatus 76
    ensis 76
    siliqua 76
Enteromorpha intestinalis 112
    linza 112
Epitonium clathrus 38
European Cowrie 34
Euspira alderia 36
    catena 36
Feather Star 104
Fucus ceranoides 126
    serratus 126
    spiralis 128
    vesiculosus 128
Furbelows 122
Gaper, Blunt 92
    Sand 92
Gaping File-Shell 66
Gari, depressa 84
    fervensis 84
    tellinella 84
Gastrana fragilis 82
Gibbula cineraria 18
    divaricata 18
    magus 16
    umbilicalis 18
Gigartina stellata 146
Glasswort 108
Glossus humanus 86
Glycymeris glycmeris 52
    pilosa 52
Goodallia triangularis 68

Grooved Razor Shell 78
Halidrys siliquosa 132
Haliotis lamellosa 8
    tuberuculata 8
Helcion laevis 14
    pellucidum 14
Heart, Shell 86
Henricia oculata 104
Hiatella arctica 94
Himanthalia elongata 136
Hinia incrassata 44
    reticulata 44
Hydrobia ulvae 26
    ventrosa 26
Ianthina exigua 38
Irish Moss 144
Irus irus 88
Lacuna vincta 22
Laevicardium crassum 70
Laminaria digitata 120
    saccharina 118
Large Sunset Shell 84
Laurencia pinnatifida 152
Laver 138
Laver Spire Shell 26
Leathesia difformis 116
Lepas anatifera 100
Lepidochitona cinereus 6
Leptochiton asellus 4
Leucophytia bidentata 50
Limaria hians 66
Limpet, American Slipper 32
    Blue-rayed 14
    Bonnet 32
    China 12
    Common 12
    Keyhole 8
    Tortoiseshell 10
    White Tortoiseshell 10
Lithophyllum incrustans 156
Littorina littorea 24
    mariae 24
    neritoides 22
    obtusata 24
    saxatilis 22
Lomentaria articulata 154
Lutraria lutraria 74
Macoma balthica 82
Mactra stultorum 74
Modiolus barbatus 56
    modiolus 56
Monodonta lineata 16
Monostroma fuscum 114
Musculus discors 54
Mussel, Bearded Horse 56
    Common 54
    Fan 58
    Horse 56
Mya arenaria 92
    truncata 92
Mytilus edulis 54
Necklace Shell, Common 36
    Large 36
Needle Shell 28

eptune Grass 106
eptunia antiqua 42
ucella lapillus 40
ucula nucleus 52
arweed 120
cenebra erinacea 40
donthalia dentata 142
rmer, Common 8
  Green 8
strea edulis 64
vatella myosotis 50
yster, Common European 64
  Common Saddle 66
  Flat 64
  Portuguese 64
  Wing 58
alliolum tigerinuma 60
almaria palmata 140
andora inaequivalvis 96
andora Shell 96
aphia rhomboides 90
aracentrotus 106
arvicardium exiguum 72
atella aspera 12
  depressa 12
  vulgata 12
ecten maximus 62
lican's Foot Shell 30
lvetia canaliculata 130
pper Dulse 152
ppery Furrow Shell 84
riwinkle, Common 24
  Flat 24
  Rough 22
  Small 22
easant Shell 20
iolas dactylus 94
ymatolithon calcareum 156
ocamium vulgare 152
lysiphonia lanosa 150
d Razor Shell 76
orphyra umbilicalis 138
sidonia oceanica 106
asiola stipitata 110
eria hirundo 58
azor Shell, Grooved 78
  Pod 76
ssoa parva 26
ccorhiza polyschides 122
cculina carcini 102
licornia europaea 108
allop, Great 62
  Queen 62
  Tiger 60
  Variegated 60
alpellum scalpellum 100
aphander lignarius 46
robicularia plana 84
ytosiphon lomentarius 134
a, Belt 118
  Hare 48
  Lace 134
  Lemon 48
  Lettuce 110

Oak 132
Potato 106
Sea-thong 136
Semibalanus balanoides 102
Sepia officinalis 98
Sepiola atlantica 98
Ship Worm 96
Solen marginatus 78
Spindle Shell 42
Spisula elliptica 74
  solida 74
Sting Winkle 40
Striaca lactea 52
Tellin, Baltic 82
  Blunt 80
  Thin 80
Teredo navalis 96
Thick Trough Shell 74
Tonicella marmorea 6
  rubra 6
Topshell, Common 20
  Flat 18
  Grey 18
  Painted 20
  Purple 18
  Thick 16
Tricolia pullus 20
Trivia artica 34
  monacha 34
Trough Shell, Elliptical 74
  Rayed 74
  Thick 74
Turritella communis 28
Tusk Shell 50
Ulva lactuca 110
Velutina velutina 34
Velvet Shell 34
Venerupis senegalensis 90
Venus, Banded 90
  Striped 90
  Warty 88
Venus verrucosa 88
Violet Sea Snail 38
Wedge Shell, Banded 78
Wentletrap, Common 38
Whelk, Common 42
  Common Dog 40
  Netted Dog 44
  Thick-lipped Dog 44
Winkle, Sting 40
  Toothed 16
Wrack, Bladder 128
  Channelled 130
  Knotted 130
  Spiral 128
  Toothed 126
  Twisted 128

Roger Phillips has pioneered the photography of natural history which ensures reliable identification. By placing each specimen against a plain background he is able to show details that would otherwise have been lost if it had been photographed solely *in situ*. Such is the success of this technique that his books, which include *Mushrooms*, *Wild Food* and *Freshwater Fish* sold over a million copies worldwide. He is also the winner of numerous awards, including three for best produced and best designed books and the André Simon prize for 1983 for *Wild Food*.

Jacqui Hurst studied photography at Gloucestershire College of Art & Design, worked as an assistant to Roger Phillips for 4 years, and is now freelance journalist and photographer, specializing in country matters.

Nicky Foy did an English degree at Queen Mary College, before training to be a teacher. After completing a one-year post-graduate degree she taught English for seven years and was Head of the Sixth Form at an inner London comprehensive. In 1982 she left teaching to become a freelance writer, researcher and editor.

Acknowledgements
We should like to thank Dr Julia Nunn for her help with the shells and Bernard Picton for the underwater photographs of living shells; also Dr Shelagh Smith for assistance with the nomenclature of the mollusca, and to the Department of Botany and Zoology, The Ulster Museum, Belfast for the loan of specimens. Finally we should like to thank J Clokie for help in finding and identifying many of the seaweeds.

Other titles in this series:

Coastal Wild Flowers

Herbs and Medicinal Plants

Wild Flowers of Roadsides and Waste Places

garden and field
Weeds

native and common
Trees

common and important
Mushrooms

woodland
Wild Flowers

First published in Great Britain 1987
by Elm Tree Books/Hamish Hamilton Ltd
27 Wrights Lane London W8 5TZ

Copyright © 1987 by Roger Phillips

Cover design by Pat Doyle

ISBN 0241-12061-6
ISBN 0241-12028-4 Pbk

Typeset by Rowland Phototypesetting Ltd
Bury St Edmunds, Suffolk
Printed in Great Britain by Cambus Litho